AND
SO
IT
IS

Bobrowitz, Gail Cheri.
And so it is / Gail Cheri Bobrowitz
ISBN 978-1-304-66025-1

Printed in the United States of America
Set in Stemple Garamond
Designed by Charles Leazott

I dedicate this story to all the strong women I know who have had the courage to change their lives and not settle for the status quo.

In particular, I think of Kim Drew Wright, who not only started a huge Women's movement but continues to work towards its goals in spite of the terrible prognosis of terminal cancer. Her humor, her intelligence and her compassion make her my Shero!

PROLOGUE

"Good morning, everyone. I am Dr. Jessica Wainsworth, the department chair of Gerontology. I want to welcome you to today's presentation of older entrepreneurs. I would like to introduce Melinda Radnor Smith. Mrs. Smith represents a part of our population which is often overlooked and marginalized, older women in business. Mrs. Smith started her first business at the age of 57, after a career teaching elementary school and raising two children. She retired from business two years ago at the age of 85. Mrs. Smith, thank you for sharing your story with us."

"Thank you, Dr. Wainsworth. Please, just call me Melinda. I agreed to tell my story today, not because I was a great entrepreneur, not because my business made a lot of money, but because too many women are subjugated to the roles they think they have to play. It's sometimes a spouse or adult children who wish to define the role they have scripted for us. I will purposefully be very detailed in relating this story. Life does not happen in a vacuum. Sometimes you are truly in control, most of the time a victim of circumstance, but I have learned that you always have a say, and your opinion is valid. I want to start back when I first came to Virginia." Melinda closed her eyes and took a deep breath.

"I came to Richmond to retire. I was in my mid-fifties and divorced. Many thought that Virginia, especially the city of Richmond, was an odd choice. The more popular locations, Florida, the Carolinas, or even Virginia Beach, would be a more logical place for a woman my age alone and in my circumstances. I didn't know a soul in Richmond, but I had always wanted to visit. It was as if something was drawing me here; something was waiting for me. I decided to follow my intuition. After all, if I hated it, I would simply leave since I had no ties or obligations. I had an idea of what I was looking for; someplace that could be a B&B, someplace that offered a relaxed setting, yet not too far off the beaten path. I wanted an area for a peaceful garden and a parking area for guests. I contacted a real estate agent, and nothing I was shown appealed to me. I got in my car and just started to drive around. I ventured further and further out of the city and ended in Chesterfield County, which is approximately 20 minutes outside of Richmond. It was an easy drive, there were several routes to get there, and although there was not that much commerce built up, there were enough places that someone could buy necessities and enjoy some restaurants. It was on one of these drives that I found a house on about 10 acres of land.

1

It was located off a secondary road and set way back on the property. Behind the house was a 40-acre tract of woods, as yet undeveloped. The location was ideal. There was a "sale by owner" sign by the driveway to the house, and I decided just to go and ring the bell. Although the people who owned the place were wary of me, they let me tour the house. It was built in 1920 and had a few additions built on over the years. Some things had been updated, and some things looked like they were original to me. A huge fireplace dominated the far wall of the living room. Surprisingly, it appeared that everything was functioning. I had a budget for the purchase and a budget for alterations and repairs. I went through the house a second time with the owners, taking notes and writing down ideas that I felt were necessary changes. The house was actually one and a half stories, with a master suite that had been added sometime recently to the first floor. There was a huge area that encompassed a kitchen, dining room, and a little office. The living room and a screened rear porch completed the downstairs. Upstairs, there were two bedrooms and a bathroom. They were not huge, but serviceable and each had adequate closet space for someone staying for a few nights or so. Although I wanted to gut the whole thing, I knew that was not reasonable. However, I saw ways to work with what was there and perhaps make changes in stages.

The price was almost within my reach, but I knew that these people really wanted to get out. I was in a great position to negotiate. I insisted on a home inspection and knew I had to get a lawyer. Arrangements were made.

I got lucky. There was nothing seriously wrong with the place, but there were many red flags that had to be addressed. Eventually, with a little haggling, and the inspection report, I was able to get the price down, waayy down. I became the owner of the property!

Living through a renovation of this magnitude on this property was a nightmare. It took far more time and money than I was prepared for. I often questioned what I had done. I am glad that I had the fortitude to stick with it."

Melinda stopped speaking for a few moments and looked around at her audience. They looked interested but a little restless. She went on, hoping to capture their full interest. Melinda once again closed her eyes and regained her composure. She then continued. "It was for no apparent reason that I took a walk that autumn day; I was not in the habit of walking in the woods. But the untamed area behind my house beckoned to me. I knew that these woods were condemned, victims of suburban growth. I had a pang of guilt, as I had taken down many trees to make way for the additions to my house. I just wanted to walk through them just once before they were gone forever. On this day though, I was feeling nostalgic for the way things must have been in the not-so-distant past. Endless miles of woods, interrupted by a system of streams, filled with birds and animals that I knew had been displaced by the advance of the suburbs. The woods were quite dense. The dried leaves crunched underfoot and released an aroma into the air as I walked. I had always avoided areas such as this, convinced that every spider, tick, and snake would be waiting for me, ready to attack and attach onto me and drain some essence out of my body. That day, I was appropriately dressed, and my desire to see this little patch of nature gave me the courage to enter into and experience the last of the wild places. Although the patch of woods was completely surrounded by heavily trafficked roads, houses, and some cleared yards, all was quiet in the interior. The world seemed to melt away, and only the sound of some late fall insects and frantic squirrels could be heard in addition to the trampling sounds I myself made. My eye caught a glimpse of something on the ground. A reflection of light bouncing off something shiny, out of place, at the base of a Hickory tree. I approached the object and saw that it was a stone, quite pretty with specks of gold and turquoise. It was out of place here. It would have been at home in the Southwest United States. Just a rock, but pleasing in its coloration and shape. It was the size of a peach pit. It appeared as if it was carved. The stone was encrusted with dirt, and I thought perhaps I could clean it up and make a piece of jewelry out of it. I placed it in my pocket, pleased that I was preserving something from this natural last stand. I continued along my walk, feeling that somehow I had accomplished something important as if I had found a buried treasure."

Melinda glanced at her audience. Now, they were following her every word. She knew this was not at all what they had expected. They were used to business people presenting ideas, business plans, and how they got financing, etc. They seemed mesmerized. "Just wait," she thought. "I am about to take you on a fantastic ride."

Melinda's eyes closed for the third time, and she continued her story as if she was watching a movie of her life.

CHAPTER ONE

Melinda was born into a time where job opportunities were just opening up for women. It was still expected that she would marry, have babies and stay home till they were school age. She was to be the smiling wife, standing at the door with the cocktail in her hand and the apron around her waist, with the statistical 2.5 clean children playing silently in an immaculate house. Yeah, right! She had married, had the kids but could never quite get the rest right. She wanted to go out into the big world that she could only watch from her kitchen window. She was educated, articulate and filled with ambition. Her husband had other ideas for her, and for some reason, probably his salary, things were done his way. Melinda did have a degree in education and a license to teach elementary school. She taught a little before her own children were born and then went to work again when the youngest was in first grade. This was considered an acceptable choice. It gave you ample vacations, short workdays, weekends, and summers. Many husbands, including hers, viewed it as the ideal second job. Not as important as their high-powered positions, just something that would occupy "the ladies" while the kids were at school themselves.

Melinda, of course, saw it differently. She took each class as a serious responsibility and felt that her contribution to society was on the same level as a physician or lawyer. Too bad she didn't have the earning power of those professions. Perhaps it was the stress of managing home and school, or perhaps it was the inherent unhappiness in the marriage, but Melinda usually felt sick. Not the kind of sick that puts you in the hospital, but a constant ache or pain or sniffles or weakness that just made most of the days miserable. The administration was not happy with her attendance record, and she was encouraged to leave her position. They admitted she always got the job done and she was very well-liked by students and faculty, but they could not handle the disruption that her poor attendance had. She regretted leaving the students and colleagues, but she had to move on.

Irreconcilable differences tore her marriage apart as well. Melinda was just not fulfilling her role as a "wife" to her husband according to Michael's way of thinking. As much as she regretted leaving her teaching position, she did not regret at all the breakup of her marriage. She liked to think that she and her ex would remain friends. The truth was that they were never really friends in the first place. She had a role to play, and her wants, dreams, and desires were never part of Michael's plans. Fortunately, Michael had a strong view that his children should want for nothing, and he provided handsomely for their needs. Custody was shared. Melinda's children were now adults and on their own. They had witnessed the psychological and verbal abuse that Melinda suffered at their father's tauntings and behavior but just thought it was part of everyday life. Sometimes, to them, it seemed funny! As they matured, they realized how abusive and cruel their father had been to their mother. The children, Dianna and Daniel, were doing well but not quite settled in their own careers and personal lives. Melinda decided not to wait for them to dictate where or what she should now do.

Her divorce settlement was generous. Michael would learn from this experience and create a prenuptial agreement in all his future marriages, but Melinda had a large cash settlement and a monthly stipend. She also had put money aside from a small inheritance from her parents.

A perk from her days married to Michael was that she had become an excellent baker and cook! She enjoyed the process and found it very creative. Her home was lovely, and she had done all the decorating work. Sometimes when looking for a project to do, she would repaint a room all by herself! She could have easily hired someone to do it, but she felt great satisfaction in doing the work herself. Of course, after such an exertion of energy, she would have increased pains and exhaustion. These skills, she felt, could always help her earn some extra cash if she had the need.

CHAPTER TWO

After almost a year, the renovations were finally completed. There had been so many changes to the original renovation plan that delays due to permits, environmental concerns, and weather extended the timeline. Melinda had opted to stay at the house during all of this. It was very difficult being isolated in the bedroom. She did not have a working kitchen, and there was constant noise and dirt generated by the construction. But she managed, with a microwave and local restaurants, and a lot of takeout! She was not used to eating this way, and even though she felt most of the time like she was starving, she was gaining weight! She occupied her time shopping for furnishings, choosing color schemes, and planning her business. It all seemed so easy because it was all ideas on paper. She hoped that the reality would not be tremendously harder to accomplish. In all this time, she had spoken regularly with her children and some friends from NY, but she was lonely. Her nagging malaise plagued her, and she hoped she had done the right thing.

She looked around at the completed job and was excited by the possibilities she saw. The kitchen, which was now truly the heart of the home, had everything she wanted and needed. There was ample cabinetry. There were deep pantries and places for her dishes and cutlery. The appliances created a professional kitchen, which could easily function as a commercial kitchen, able to cater dinners to large groups. She finally had enough oven space with two commercial ovens to put out displays of cookies, muffins, cakes, and pies that she had quite a reputation for. Two large dishwashers were installed. The appliances were all stainless steel, the cabinetry white, the original wide plank wood floor just added warmth to the industrial style of the kitchen. There was a large kitchen island with a sink and plenty of room to roll out dough or set up a buffet. She couldn't wait to get busy cooking here. The dining room was set up perpendicular to the kitchen island. There was plenty of space separating the two rooms, even though they were open to each other. The table had the ability to expand, creating room for 20 guests when needed, but when closed, it comfortably would seat 10. There was a little eating nook, where the small office used to be, for a quick informal meal. It was really a cozy corner where Melinda planned to eat most of her meals and set up a little coffee bar for B&B guests to grab a snack when the business would be up and running.

The rest of the house had been updated. The biggest addition was the construction of a three-car garage off the kitchen, with a self-contained apartment on top of it. The garage attached to the house through a new office and Melinda installed a large laundry area. This would take care of her personal needs as well as the towels and linens generated by her guests.

Upstairs in the main house, the bedrooms were reconfigured to give each one more space. A second bath was added so that each room had an ensuite. The new apartment backed up to the second floor but was not accessible from the upstairs.

Back at the entrance, space was taken from a coat closet to create a powder room so that people wouldn't have to run upstairs to use the bathroom. The front of the property had a new circular driveway. Guests could drive to the front door, then proceed around to designated parking spaces. The landscaper she hired, Hendricks, cleaned up the front and created a little garden in the center of the curve created by the driveway. One day she thought she would love to add a fountain in the center. Melinda had seen Hendricks all over the neighborhood, and he seemed to be doing a great job. Melinda loved flowers and colorful plants, but she hated taking care of them. An irrigation system for the area closest to the property was installed to water the plants and flowers that Hendricks would place along the base of the B&B. The rear of the property, now with a new patio, was kept as natural as possible. A few benches were placed on the edge of the cleared areas. Melinda thought that perhaps she could add some bird feeding stations to attract more birds to the property. That would wait till the spring. She had thought about enclosing the screened porch off of her bedroom but decided to leave it alone for now.

With all the workmen gone, the house was so quiet. Melinda walked through every room, happy with the outcome. The decor was as she imagined. The bathrooms were pristine, even though basic, the common areas inviting, and her bedroom an oasis.

Just when she thought she was finished, she realized she needed insurance and smoke detectors. She knew that was necessary in order to have paying guests. As soon as she thought of it, it was accomplished within a week. The security was minimal, but Melinda rationalized that it was enough to start with. With another Thanksgiving approaching, and no one coming for the holiday, Melinda set out to stock the pantry and use her new kitchen for the first time to sharpen her skills. She made a list, had to go to Costco, and 3 supermarkets to complete the list. It took hours to put everything away and create a plan of what she was going to cook and bake. It was at this point that she took a walk through the woods behind her house, perhaps to fortify herself for the actual start of a B&B.

CHAPTER THREE

Stanford Wingate III sat in his office finishing up some last-minute calculations. Fridays were his least favorite day. This particular Friday in November, with the sun setting and pink and purple streaks slashed across the sky, had him wondering what he was going to eat, do, and plan for Saturday. It seemed as if the whole world looked forward to the weekend, but all Stan wanted to do was go home, have his normal routine, and report to work the next day. He knew he had no life. He was just resigned to it. He thought about Saturday. He could shop, but he didn't need anything. He thought about dinner and knew that he would just heat up some canned soup. Stan only had one focus, and that was his job. He was a sterling employee. All his time, energy and loyalty were devoted to the job. He had come right out of college into this firm. He was a CPA and had advanced as far as he could. His lack of upward mobility made his employer very content. Stan was satisfied with his salary, loved a big workload, and best of all, no one at the office ever bothered with him. In fact, hardly anyone who worked there even knew his name. Just the way he wanted it!

He checked the clock, knew that he was finished for the day, and gathered the papers he was working on. He tidied up his desk, grabbed his coat and attaché case and locked his office door. He made his way to the elevator, entered and descended down to the lobby floor. Stan didn't need a car. He lived in an apartment building about half a mile from the office. He enjoyed the walk home, no matter what the weather. He did, however, own a car, leased it actually, and drove it rarely. His usual destinations were to visit his mother, now firmly placed in an assisted living facility, or on occasion, take a ride into the countryside. He never stopped anywhere, never made a purchase, or spoke to anyone.

As he walked home today, he thought as he often did about his life situation. Stanford was the miracle baby of his day. His Mother and Father had been married 15 years without successfully conceiving a child. Mother was most distraught, as the story goes. She felt it was her responsibility to have a son carry on the Wingate name. She was not particularly maternal. She had pictured a baby nurse followed by a nanny attending to her children. They would be dressed in the finest clothes and always demonstrating the manners of Southern gentility. The doctors in the 1950s were learning much about infertility, but the gains of modern medicine of that decade would not be available to Mother. Miraculously, when all hope of conceiving was given up, she accomplished a viable pregnancy. Mother stayed on bed rest for the remainder of the 9 months and then gave birth to a very small but healthy baby boy. His parents were so thrilled that they had finally fulfilled their obligation. Now they would leave the rest of it up to hired help. Stanford grew up in the lap of luxury. He had everything a child could want except for the affection and interaction with his parents. Father was killed in a bizarre accident when Stanford was 11. The only memories he had of the man were his formality, his bigoted views on race and religion, and his love for the game of chess!

Now, at the age of 47, Stanford was his mother's caretaker. Just as he was raised, he, in turn, left the total responsibility of her care to strangers. They were well paid and provided benefits. The environment in which she lived was clean and lovely. He dutifully visited for one hour each week. It didn't really matter; she didn't know who he was or how often he came. They rarely spoke or interacted. He was certain, though, he was being a good son. Stanford believed that one particular facet of his life kept him apart from the rest of the world. If only he weren't so short! He knew it sounded ridiculous, but for a man, 5'3, life was cruel. He felt he always fell short of any mark! What woman would look at him? There wasn't a place he could go to without short jokes or jeers. He had tried all confidence boosters. He had tried to meet people through church or clubs. He never followed through, fearing the rejection that he had encountered all his life. He decided just to be grateful that he had what he had, and for some reason, he was not deserving for anymore. He blamed his mother for the negative messages she sent him as a child, he blamed his classmates for picking on him, he blamed his teachers for not supporting him. He blamed everyone else, but for what he was not sure. Today, he knew that children in similar situations had medical options to correct growth hormone imbalance. For him, it was too late, and a little man was all he could ever be

It was really a cruel joke. He was born into an old Virginia family that could trace their lineage back to the founding fathers of the Old Dominion, and before that, to England. He had a proud heritage. Although his ancestors were on the losing side of the "War of Northern Aggression," it was known that they were an honorable upstanding family and found their place again in the upper socioeconomic class of the New South. His great grandfathers, grandfather, and father were all prominent business leaders and dabbled in politics. One could say, "big men." Now there was just him. Just him and dear old Mother.

CHAPTER FOUR

Aviva spent her morning at the white elephant sale. She was in good spirits knowing that she had collected $350 for the school through the sale of the biggest collection of junk she had ever seen. People were very generous this time. Past sales had not been that profitable. It was important, she felt, that the school raise enough money to equip the new computer lab. It had taken many months of planning and many different avenues of fundraising to reach the $30,000 for the renovation and electrical upgrade to support the lab equipment.

Aviva was a huge proponent of the technical growth of the school even though she was aware that most of the children had PCs at home, and they probably knew more about how to operate the machines than she did. She also knew that once the lab was up and functioning, so many safeguards would be put in place to keep the outside world from intruding into the closed atmosphere of the Yeshiva. Modern Yeshivas such as this were really quite a contradiction. The administration wanted all the children to know HOW to operate and make use of the computer's power, but they also wanted the children to refrain from communicating with any stranger at the same time. Many of the children had homes completely closed to the outside world. No TV, radio tuned to one station that reported news from Israel, and carefully selected newspapers and screened computers. The children grew in a caring and loving environment but were insulated to see only their own community. The outside world, visible all around their ghetto mentality community, was a complete mystery constantly beckoning but completely forbidden to them. They were taught that they were special. Chosen by God to perform their religious duties and be the strength of Israel. The others, which meant all others, were to be respected but not trusted, dealt with at a minimum, and ignored in all their customs and habits. The others, also Children of God, were just a notch or two below the exalted position which the Almighty had bestowed upon them. Therefore they had to safeguard their position in the world and try not to let anyone else in. Conversion was allowed but discouraged.

Any convert, no matter how "frum" (religious and observant), would always be a fringe member of their society. The religious message, filled with the wisdom of the ages, the commitment to life and the accent on charity and education, was often lost in the minutiae of detail and the desire to outdo one's neighbor in the appearance of orthodoxy. The majority of the people followed the countless rules and regulations, recited passages in a language long extinct that they only had a slight understanding of, and practiced traditions that no longer made sense. The sexist roles, the ancient taboos, the closed society were accepted as the way things had to be. Change, if any, was a tedious and very slow process. Yet, they had managed to exist for over 5,700 years despite extreme prejudice and countless attacks against them. Just for that, they had to be admired.

Aviva, although committed to this community and religion, had numerous curiosities about the world. She had a desire to experience for herself what was out there. The problem was that she was too afraid to make any move that would put her outside the accepted confines of her environment. The pull between there and here haunted her daily. Perhaps if she were happy with her life, completely happy, the attraction of the non-Jewish orthodox world would not seem to call her so. Her sadness stemmed from her relationship with her husband and her unfulfilled sexual frustration. She found it funny that women were supposed to be pure and go to their wedding bed free from any sexual knowledge or experience. The young grooms knew no more than the brides but expected sexual pleasure and satisfaction.

In most cases, wedding nights were a disaster. In this community, it is forbidden for men and women to even touch before marriage. The combination of fear and the unknown resulted in an embarrassing exchange that was quickly accomplished. As time went by, couples developed a routine that gave little satisfaction to both parties. Men had more latitude to experiment, and many did. They would resort to clandestine affairs outside the community. Some men would take it even further and find biblical evidence to support concubines to satisfy their sexual appetites. Women, married women especially, were left to cope with their frustrations and dreams and substitute sex with the rigors of raising children. In most cases, many children.

Aviva had been raised to believe that it was her sacred duty to deal with her husband the best she knew how, but she craved affection and satisfaction that just wasn't there. She had never strayed from the philosophy and teachings of her religion, but there was a growing, swelling craving that she felt was starting to overwhelm her. She approached her husband from several angles, from conversation to teasing play. There was no apparent interest on his part. He performed his duty to his wife and seemed unaware that anything more could exist. In time, her desire for him started to wane, but the desire for physical pleasure and emotional closeness expanded, covering her and suffocating her.

CHAPTER FIVE

"November in Richmond is a magical time," she thought out loud. Melinda stood in her kitchen staring out the window, the morning light splashing into the kitchen recesses. The spectacular color of the trees, the reds, and golds most noticeable. The air had just a touch of coolness, a slight breeze wrestling the drying leaves still on the trees outside. She was entranced by the natural beauty and thought to herself how nice it was to have the autumn season last so long here. She shook herself out of her daydreaming and picked up the odd stone she had placed in her pocket a few days earlier. As she started to wash off the dirt, she smiled and said, "Why isn't there a genie in here to grant me a wish?" With anticipation, she waited for a reply or a puff of smoke or something to happen. When all remained the same, she smiled again and said to the stone, "I choose to believe that you have magical powers, so here is my wish... I wish all my wishes could be answered and that the supply was unlimited." The stone, still unresponsive, became more beautiful when clean. Melinda decided to keep in on the window ledge above the kitchen sink so that she could be reminded of her wishes every day. The sun seemed to enhance the specks of gold in the stone. The blue hues seemed to deepen. It really was a most unusual rock. She dried her hands, and as she walked out of the kitchen, stated, "I love this place, but it is so very lonely."

The weather forecast didn't seem to coincide with the picture outside. The meteorologist was talking about a large area of low pressure and Arctic air heading towards central Virginia. The change was to occur by late afternoon, the evening hours looking wet and bleak. There was concern that this low would hang around for the next day or two before it would dry out and return the temperatures to a more moderate level. Melinda decided that she needed a project if she was going to be stuck inside. With Thanksgiving just a couple of weeks away, she planned to spend the inclement weather baking and preparing some chicken and beef stock. Not that she had plans for the holiday. Her children were involved in their own activities and wouldn't be able to come to Richmond. They had both promised to come at Christmas, but she wasn't holding her breath. She smiled to herself, thinking how she had pushed to make sure that her son and daughter were strong and independent people. She wanted to protect them from the feelings of panic and inadequacy that she had had when her marriage fell apart. She only held on to her identity and sanity because she had the kids to take care of. If she had been on her own, she was sure she would have collapsed into a ball of anxiety and self-pity. It was bittersweet that she had accomplished raising two strong independent people who seemed to have little sentimentality for a holiday that means so much to their mother!

The science of meteorology is far from perfect. This time it was right on target. The golden morning sunshine had grown steadily grayer. By the afternoon, the skies were an angry gray-brown, and the wind had started to pick up speed. The trees danced at an ever-faster pace, and the dried leaves were caught up in the tempo. The sky was filled with floating specks of color as the leaves, desperate to hang on, were ripped from their hold on the branches. It was a furious collision of red, brown and yellow. Inside, Melinda was clanging pots and pans. She had purchased all the ingredients for several batches of muffins, pies, and cookies. She had bought a ton of chicken for stock and salad. She was planning out what to start first and how she would pack and freeze the finished products. The stock, cookies, and pies could be frozen for 2 months or so without any ill effects. Muffins always tasted a little funny to her if frozen for too long. She was busy organizing her plan of attack as the rain started to fall. The days were naturally shorter now, but today the sky turned black exceptionally early as the rain pelted the house at an alarming speed. Melinda turned the volume of the boombox high with her CDs she called cooking music. She chose oldies to which she could hum along and not mind when the noise of the blender or mixer would drown out the song selection. She knew the Boom Box was old school, but she had an emotional attachment to it and knew how to operate it! Before long, the kitchen was filled with steam and sounds of sizzle. The chopping, cooking, boiling, steaming, frying, melting, mixing all taking place in each preparation. With the precision of a chef in a fine restaurant, Melinda accomplished one task and went on to the next. Finally, hours later, feet aching from standing too long, everything was either finished and cooling or simmering until perfectly done. It was then that Melinda turned off the boom box and became aware of a scratching noise. The sound seemed to be coming from the rear screened porch. She was frightened by the unfamiliar sound. After putting on outdoor lights and illuminating the porch itself, Melinda looked from the family room window that had a view of the area. The rain was being carried by the wind at a 45-degree angle. It was one of the nastiest nights Melinda could remember. Again, the noise and then something more. It sounded like a cry, a whimper. She couldn't see anything more from this angle. She put on a sweatshirt over her t-shirt and jeans and opened the interior door to the porch. She looked around and saw nothing and then the sound again, and the whimper from the porch door to the garden. Without thinking of any consequence, Melinda opened the door, and a frightened, soaking wet dog stared at her with pleading eyes. "What are you doing out on a terrible night like this puppy? Come on in." She motioned with her hands to come into the porch, and the dog didn't wait for a second invitation. As the dog stood in the center of the enclosed area, it shook off all the excess water that it could shed. The resulting spray hitting Melinda with cold pin-like sensations. "Well, thanks a lot!" she said, "Next time, I will bring an umbrella to protect myself!" She told the dog to stay, although there was little reason to do so, and went back inside to get a towel. When Melinda returned, she wrapped the dog in the towel and gently started to dry the animal. She determined the dog was female and started questioning why she would be running around on such an inhospitable night. The dog was a good listener and, as expected, didn't reply. As Melinda was finishing the good rub-dry job, she noticed the dog's nostrils sniffing at the aromas emanating from the kitchen.

"Okay," said Melinda, I will be happy to give you a good meal if you promise me that you are housebroken and have done everything for the night because I am NOT walking you later! You can eat and spend the night on the porch out of the rain, but that's as far as things go. Understood?" The dog looked at her as if she understood and then turned her head towards the kitchen again.

Melinda led the dog into the warmth of the house, cut up some of the cooking chicken and broth and watched the dog gobble it down. With an expression of gratitude on her face, the dog came over to Melinda and rubbed its face against her leg. Melinda laughed and said, "Next time, use a napkin!"

Since everything in the house was new, Melinda had no old blanket or old carpet remnant for the pooch. She took some of the towels from one of the guest rooms and made a makeshift bed for the dog. She thought to herself that at least she could launder the towels without resorting to buying new ones. She placed the dog bed on the rear porch and led the dog to the designated spot, leaving her there in the shelter from the rain, but not the wind and cold. Melinda put an old mixing bowl filled with water in the corner of the porch as well. Melinda said goodnight, turned off the rear lights and locked the interior door. About 10 minutes later, it started. The pathetic cries! Melinda relented and opened the door to calm the dog when she was assaulted by the wind, her maternal instincts getting the better of her. "Okay, I'm coming," she said to no one in particular. She opened the door widely to find the dog waiting with what only could be described as a smile on its face. The dog followed her into the bedroom, waiting until she locked up the door and turned off the exterior light. Once inside the bedroom, Melinda closed the bedroom door to keep the dog from roaming through the other rooms. "Goodnight," She once again gave warning about messing anything up.

In the morning, Melinda awoke from a pleasant dream to find the dog curled up against her legs on the bed. The dog sensing the transition between sleep and awake stretched out on her back, all four legs in the air, gave a big yawn and then turned over and wiggled her way under Melinda's arm. "Do you like to cuddle in the morning, huh?" Melinda thought that this was the most delightful way she had awakened in years!

"Don't get too comfortable," Melinda said, "I don't want a dog. I don't want the responsibility of a dog, and no matter how cute you think you are, you are not my dog! In fact, today we start the search for your family. Someone must be missing you."

Even though the dog had no tag or collar, Melinda was sure that such a cute dog must have a family. Before she could say more, the dog jumped off the bed, indicated she wanted the bedroom and porch door opened, and for the lack of a better word, asked to be let out! Not knowing what else to do, Melinda complied, and the dog went running out to the trees, took less than a minute and headed back into the house feeling totally relieved. Melinda had hardly had time to go into the house herself.
"Well, okay, you can stay but only until we find your family."
As if the dog understood but didn't care, she walked back inside and made herself comfortable by the kitchen table. Melinda laughed to herself, "I bet you are waiting for breakfast, eh?

CHAPTER SIX

Melinda sat in the waiting area of Dr. John's Pet Hospital. Sitting obediently at her side was the pooch. After two weeks of posters with the dog's description and her phone number, countless phone calls to animal agencies, and every veterinarian in the area, no one had come forth to claim the dog. As much as she fought against adopting the dog herself, she couldn't seem to give it up for adoption. Melinda realized that she needed to call the dog something, give it a meaningful name. After considering several choices, Melinda went to the Thesaurus and looked under solo. The dog had arrived at her home alone or solo. Solo was discarded as a name because it sounded too masculine. She found a note that said, "see unity" and turned the pages till the word appeared. Under the third category, adjectives, it said, "one, sole, lone, single, odd, individual, singular, unique." The dog seemed to fit into this category, for she came alone; she was quite individualistic and unique. " Unity it is." Melinda had proclaimed to the dog. During these last two weeks, Melinda had purchased a collar, leash, doggy dish, grooming brush, and doggie food treats. Melinda didn't want to admit that she had fallen completely and totally in love with the animal. She had fought with herself every step of the way and with every purchase. She convinced herself that the dog's owner would come forth and that she would be stuck with all this dog paraphernalia, but each day she also dreaded getting a response from her inquiries. Now, two weeks later and Thanksgiving a day away, Melinda had a permanent border to share the big house with her. The beautiful young dog, tricolor, of brown, beige, and black, seemed to adjust to her new surroundings as if she knew she was to be there with Melinda all along.

Melinda had chosen this particular veterinarian because he had been so supportive and helpful as she searched for the owners of Unity. Although he was not the closest vet around, Melinda had a good feeling about him and figured the trip was not that far, and Unity deserved the best!

Charlene Adams was busily talking on her cellphone. The conversation seemed agitated. Two cats in pet carriers were impervious to the owner's heated discussion. As Charlene ended the conversation on the phone, she yelled "SHIT" louder than she expected. Feeling embarrassed, she turned to Melinda and said, "I know there must be a reason why this just happened, but I am truly at a loss to know what it is! I have guests coming in from out of town for Thanksgiving. I had made reservations for them at a charming bed and breakfast. I just received word that it was damaged by a water main break this morning and won't be able to accommodate them! I have to hunt around now for something, a motel, I guess, far less attractive and, I'm sure, expensive due to the holiday. As soon as I finish here with the cats, I better get my ass in gear and find the rooms."

Melinda questioned, "How many people are you expecting?"
"Four adults. They are coming up from Atlanta for two nights," she answered.
Out of nowhere, Melinda found herself saying, "I have a huge home and just Unity and I live there. I was thinking about starting some sort of B&B myself. Why don't you come over and take a look at it now? I think you would find it most appealing for your friends!"

Melinda was surprised to say this, but Charlene felt she now knew the reason for the incident.
"Are you sure? How much would you charge?" asked Charlene.
"No, I'm not sure, but I'll never know unless I try." "Hi." She said, extending her hand, " My name is Melinda, and this is my dog Unity."
"Great to meet you, Melinda. I'm Charlene Adams."

CHAPTER SEVEN

A new computer sat in Aviva's home. Her children had presented it to her, along with their father, for her birthday. Aviva's children were now 21 years old. The triplets, two boys and a girl, were finishing studies at Yeshiva University in New York City. Chaim was going on to study law, Yosef was headed for the financial world, and Tova would teach, as her mother did before her.

Knowing that mom was experiencing the first pull of the empty nest, the children had decided to give her the new computer to provide her with hours and hours of activity. Little did they know that her hours of activity would take such a bizarre twist.

Aviva had chosen AOL as her internet provider. She had a good working knowledge of the computer but had used it only in an academic manner. As she sat home one afternoon, alone in the house, she decided to play around with the machine and have some exploratory fun. She investigated the chatrooms, made a personal profile, including her religious orthodoxy, and chose the screen name, "2lifelady." As she was playing around, learning the ins and outs of her new machine, she received an instant message. The screen name of "Eaglesfly12" greeted her with a simple hello. Curious, although cautious about replying, she went ahead and responded in kind. The gentleman at the other end of the conversation said he was just doing a member search and was fascinated by the information she had included in her profile. There was nothing threatening about the conversation. There was nothing suggestive about the comments, and the time passed by quickly. When Aviva realized she had spent three hours "talking" to this person, she became flustered. She told Eagle she had to get off the computer but that it was lovely speaking with him. He suggested that they buddy list each other and that perhaps they could talk again sometime. With that accomplished, they both said goodbye. Aviva quickly signed offline, turned off her computer and ran around the kitchen trying to get dinner ready.

In the weeks that followed, every spare minute Aviva could get, she would sign on and look for Eagle. More often than not, they would find each other. It seems he had a computer at his disposal at work, and he could use it anytime he wished, as he owned his own business and answered to no one. The timbre of the conversations had gone from friendly to very personal. Eagle told her of his yearnings, his loneliness; he always said things with respect, nothing ever vulgar or dirty. He went into deep insights about relationships. They spoke together of the religious world and the secular. He assured her that she was the most understanding woman he had ever encountered and that he could feel her anguish, her pain over her unfulfilled marriage. He told her that her anxiety over her children leaving the home was normal, her desires for the unknown understandable but dangerous. He counseled her to beware of people online, although indeed, as she already knew, she could trust him. She never realized that she was being manipulated by a master. Within two months, Aviva thought she was in love. Online conversations now extended to phone conversations. The words he spoke now had a voice, and that voice was beautiful. He fed her dreams, and she felt that she had someone with whom she could really communicate everything with. He made her feel intelligent, witty, and sexy. Somewhere along the way, much of the conversation had turned sexual. Not a pornographic type of sexual, but rather a wishful thinking expression. He would tell her that if he were with her, he would take the time to please her. He described things he would do to her that made the inside of her body warm and a delicious feeling grow in her groin. She sometimes wanted to touch herself as they talked but felt embarrassed that she would even consider such a thing. It was only a matter of time that she HAD to meet him, face to face. He suggested a public place, middle of the afternoon. He told her to write down his real name and business address, place them in an envelope. On the outside of the envelope, she should write, "if anything ever happens to me, open this letter." In addition, she should list the time and date they were to meet. The envelopes should be kept in a safe place that " G-D forbid " anything should ever happen to her, her family would know where to look, or better yet, give the envelope to a trusted friend. Unfortunately, there was no one to who Aviva felt she could entrust the envelope. She decided to place it in the safe, knowing that under normal conditions, her husband would never open the safe, but if something should happen to her, he would go there immediately.

At the first meeting, Aviva thought she would vomit; she was so scared. She went anyway. The hours of conversation, confidences, tears and giggles drove her to meet this man no matter what the consequences may be. She kept telling herself that this was a harmless meeting, that she knew him so well already, what could possibly happen?

At times like this, Aviva wished she could just speak with her friend Melinda. Although Melinda was quite a bit older, she was the only non-Orthodox Jewish woman she knew. The two had met years earlier while they were both teaching. The public elementary school was located perpendicular to the Yeshiva building. Parking was a huge problem as neither school had parking provided for teachers and staff. Each day, the two sets of faculty would vie for insufficient street parking.

19

On top of that, the location of the schools put them in the highest car theft area of NYC. It seemed as if Melinda and Aviva were always arriving at their respective schools at the same time and trying to outmaneuver each other for a spot. After a while, they recognized each other and made a plan. They would meet in two cars ten blocks away, where parking was not an issue. They took turns weekly, parking one car there and taking the other to find the elusive school spot. They figured that they would have better luck searching for one spot instead of fighting each other for two. Over a few months, they exchanged phone numbers in case one was ill or not showing up at school for other reasons, and they started to have conversations. Eventually, they would meet half an hour earlier to have coffee and chat before they would begin their teaching day.

How Aviva missed Melinda. She was her inspiration, her link to the outside world. She, of course, had her new address in Virginia and the phone number, but it just wasn't the same as those in-person talks.

Aviva spotted Eagle standing just where he said he would be. She had her breath taken away at the fact that he was really good-looking and had not exaggerated his appearance. He, too, knew exactly who she was. Their public meeting would last only 15 minutes. The overwhelming desire to be alone with this man won over her conviction to keep it simple and safe. They went to his office; no one else would be there.

All her married life, Aviva had thought sex was an obligation. She also thought that she was to blame for the lack of sensation she felt during sex. Now, a miracle! In two hours, this man, this wonderful man, had shown her what it was all about. She was in a state of disbelief and shame. She felt exhilarated and embarrassed. She tried hard to convince herself that she was apart from her body, watching the action from the sidelines as if taking notes for a documentary. No matter how hard she tried to imagine being an observer, she knew that she had been the star participant. All of a sudden, a terrible realization came over her. She was dirty. She had broken a commandment, and she was beside herself with fear.

She ran to the Mikvah, the ritual bath, to cleanse herself. It wasn't the right time of the month for her, so she went to one of the baths in a different neighborhood. The Mikvah lady there would not question her motive for the visit. She wasn't sure if this would cleanse her sins, but she was hesitant to ask the guidance of the Rabbi. She knew this indiscretion, this one blissful experience, had changed her forever. She also knew she wanted it again and again, but it HAD to stop.

CHAPTER EIGHT

Charlene Adams, a nice-looking middle-aged woman, was a native of Richmond, Virginia. As a child, she attended the right schools and the right church, but by the age of 13, she was totally disenchanted by the teachings that were being forced upon her. In an act of defiance, she refused to attend either Sunday school or church in her teenage years. Her desire to flee from the confines of Richmond was realized at the age of 18 when she and a childhood male friend decided to marry and leave their hometown. Neither one of them had any idea of what to expect, where to settle, or how to make enough money to support themselves. Just the acute need to get out of Richmond propelled them, and they ultimately ended up in California. Within a few years, the marriage was over, and the realities of life were setting in. Charlene found employment and took night classes in a junior college, looking for a direction in her life. She developed an interest in law and set on a path to be a paralegal. Diligently she worked her way into a degree and a "real" job in her field. When she got her feet back on the ground, she re-established a relationship with her mother back in Virginia. Life choices created many moves for Charlene; she lived in different cities, states and always felt restless with the choices. She had a couple more failed marriages, and eventually, depression set in as she felt incapable of ever finding happiness. One day, a friend at work suggested to her that she should come to church on Sunday. With a laugh, Charlene explained in no uncertain terms that she "didn't do church."

"This isn't anything like the churches you went to back home," the friend replied, "Just give it one chance, I know, really know, that you will find something there for you."

Charlene answered, "The first time someone mentions God, I'm out of there."

Charlene smiled to herself as she remembered the conversation more than 20 years ago. She often thought about the first Sunday when she was almost dragged into the "church" building, which was nothing more than a store in a strip mall. She recalled how she was on guard that this was a cult, waiting to get another body in their clutches. What she found was a philosophy, a way of life, a clearer picture of who she was in her relationship to every other human being on the planet. What she found was Religious Science. She not only went to church that Sunday but became a regular. She attended classes to understand more of the relationship between man and God, the wisdom contained in other religious philosophies and the laws of science

21

and how they govern our lives. This led to further study and culminated in a ministerial decree. When she was ready to leave the learning phase, although one never stops learning, and go on to the teaching phase, without hesitation, she chose to return to Richmond. She found out that there was a very small group that existed there, without a minister and the opportunity to "grow" a church was filled with expectation. Before she left California, she married once more to a man who shared her ambition, philosophy, and desires. That was five years ago. To Charlene, it was the happiest 5 years of her life. Her "church" had only minimally grown in the five years since she was here, but her vision for the church never wavered. There is a steady core of 50 or so members, but Charlene knew that a growth explosion was just around the corner.

Charlene Adams wasn't surprised that Melinda had offered her home to her out-of-town guests. It was something meant to be that placed Melinda and Charlene together in the vet's office. The two women concluded their business with their animals. Charlene followed Melinda in her own car back to the newly designated Bed and Breakfast. Charlene was impressed with the first view. The home was large, and everything inside and out looked like it came out of a swanky magazine. The upstairs rooms that would be reserved for guests were ample in size, and each had its own bath and closet space. The furnishings in each bedroom had two twin-size beds pushed together to look like a king-size. Also a dresser, night table, lamps, a comfortable chair, and a side table in each room. Each room was painted a different color and decorated with corresponding fabrics and pillows. They were both beautiful. Walls were decorated with tasteful art. Each bathroom had coordinated towels and floor mats plus toilet articles that were pieces of art themselves. The bedrooms were all carpeted. Melinda didn't stop with the future guest quarters. She showed Charlene the whole house, delighted in doing so. Charlene was her very first visitor, not counting Unity, of course!

"And here in the kitchen," Melinda rambled, "here are some of my favorite toys." Melinda showed her professional range, double ovens big enough to cook for a party of 20 without any problem, and a tremendous Sub-zero refrigerator. It seemed to Charlene that every imaginable gadget had a place in Melinda's kitchen.

"I have an extra fridge and freezer in the garage. I don't know why exactly, but it's in there should I need it. In addition, the little apartment above the garage has a mini kitchen, and don't forget the wet bar in my sitting room."

"This place is fabulous. What will you charge for each night?" Charlene asked.

"Let me think, Ummm, what were they going to pay in the other place?" Inquired Melinda.

"It was $85 per night, and that included breakfast," answered Charlene. "Breakfast? Is that a full breakfast or just a continental breakfast?"

"I'm pretty sure it was a full breakfast, but don't worry about it. You weren't prepared for something like this."

Melinda laughed, "I am always prepared for something like this. I have everything anyone would want for breakfast, well, almost everything. I am sure your guests will be satisfied. Let's just say, $70 per night per room, and a full breakfast included if they want it. Maybe before or after a Thanksgiving dinner, they would want to keep it light. No matter, whatever they want, I can prepare it."

Charlene replied, "Sounds great, but Thanksgiving dinner is just a restaurant deal. My husband and I have a small place down in the city, and I don't particularly care to cook, so we are just thrilled to have our friends here, and we will take them out to eat. They are used to it, most of them feel the same way. They are other couples we met when I was studying to be a minister."

"Minister?" Melinda was surprised.

"Yup! I am Reverend Charlene," she said, laughing.

"What church?" asked Melinda.

"Religious Science" was the answer.

"I never heard of it, and I thought I knew most of them," said Melinda

"Well, anytime you want to know more, you know where to find me." Charlene booked the rooms, and the women exchanged business cards. Charlene told her to expect evening guests.

"They're renting a car at the airport, and then they will come directly to my house. Then they'll follow me here. We should be here somewhere about three. I guess we'll hang out and go out for a light bite early, then we have some catching up to do and some business to conduct. Do you think we could do that hereafter our dinner?" Charlene was hopeful that Melinda would say yes.

"That's fine. You can use the family room or one of the rooms upstairs if you choose." Melinda realized for the first time that being a B&B meant sharing your whole home with your guests.

Before the women concluded the house tour, Charlene caught a glimpse of the shiny stone on the windowsill.

"What is that?" she asked as she pointed to the stone.

" It's interesting, isn't it?" replied Melinda. "I found it one day walking around the woods, and it just seemed to call to me. I love the way it radiates light."

Both women walked away from the encounter with a good feeling. Melinda looked at Unity, who was curled up on the kitchen floor, "Looks like we are in business." Unity seemed unfazed.

CHAPTER NINE

Stanford dressed for Thanksgiving dinner, all the while convincing himself that the time spent at the assisted living was going to be a hellish affair. The dinner will be passable, he was sure, but the companionship of Mother and the other residents would almost be unbearable. From past experience, he knew that the headache he would suffer would start somewhere around dessert and grow into a migraine through the night. He tried to prepare himself to relax. After all, these people weren't really responsible any longer for the things they said and did. He should be more compassionate, acknowledge their limitations and realize that someday he might be in the same condition. "I will put a bullet in my head first!" he declared out loud.

He knew he had an obligation to go. It was Mother, after all, and being an only child made demands on him. Mother would forget 2 minutes after the dinner that he was there at all. He, however, would know that he shirked a responsibility if he skipped the dinner. That would bother him for days, instead of the hours that headache would last, till the medication would kick in. Stoically, silently, he would accept his responsibility.

His experience that night proved to be true. As anticipated, he came home with head pounding, nausea gripping his chest and enormous sensitivity to light. He swallowed the analgesic tablets and ripped off the clothes he was wearing as if they were offending items. He crawled into bed, praying for sleep to remove him from the misery of his present condition. He tried to create mental scenarios taking him to calm and pleasant places. His imagination failed him, for he was so pathetically out of practice and its use. It was at least four hours later that sleep finally claimed victory over his mental and physical torture.

In sleep, the realm of the subconscious, Stan was free to dream. He could see a sculptor working on a large stone, delicately chipping away at a form. The artist had his face shielded from the flying fragments as he chipped away into the rock. Slowly, the form started to take shape, and Stan saw himself. He was stiff, unbending, and it seemed as if life could exist below the surface. Yes, there is a definite sign of life in the rock, but Stan was immovable. The artist continued to chip away, slowly, each stroke causing more debris to lift away. In the end, he could almost see his whole self, but life never seemed to bubble to the surface. Chip, chip, chip, the tools would dig into the rock, exposing more of Stan, the rhythmic tempo, the click of the metal tools, the chunks of rock.

Stan awoke, feeling the chipping in his head but the intensity of the pain subsiding. He recalled the dream as he entered the shower but quickly dismissed reading any meaning into it, for that would mean he would have to face himself, and he couldn't bear it.

CHAPTER TEN

"Welcome to Hickory Acres!" Melinda greeted the guests as they entered the house.

"Hickory Acres?" Charlene looked quizzical.

"I needed a name for the newly established business, and I looked around. I realized that a great deal of the trees on the property are Hickory trees, hence the name." Melinda was beaming. She was so excited. Introductions were made all around, and the guests went upstairs to choose their rooms and drop off their bags. Unity had come to the front door to meet the guests too. She stood at Melinda's side, and as each person entered the foyer, the dog sniffed the air. Apparently, they all met with Unity's approval, for the dog soon departed and took the place she had adopted as her designated spot at the entrance to Melinda's bedroom suite. Melinda had taken out a beautiful guest registry book. It really was an empty journal that someone had given her as a gift when she retired. She had never made an entry, and the cover had suggested to her that this would be a better use than her ramblings about what she did on a daily basis. She had busied herself before the people arrived by freshening up the rooms on the second floor, making sure all was in order and then coming downstairs to remove muffins and pastries from the freezer. She had brewed a pot of coffee and prepared some fresh chocolate chip cookies as well. She also had readied all the ingredients for a country breakfast for Thanksgiving morning. Hickory Acres looked fabulous, aromas of fresh baked goods emanated from the kitchen, and the smile was still firmly upon Melinda's face.

Melinda met Charlene's husband, Ken, as well as the B&B's first guests. They sat down in the family room and helped themselves to some coffee and cookies.

She watched her guests as they chatted incessantly. They were already having a good time, filling each other in on their personal lives, giggling about past experiences and playfully teasing each other. This was hardly what Melinda would have expected from six people, where four of them happened to be ministers. The relationship of these friends was warm and energetic. They seemed so easy with one another, not at all preachy as she had imagined. As she cleaned up from the impromptu snack, the group ascended upstairs. Melinda realized that she was really unprepared to be a B&B hostess from the business point of view. If she was really going to get into this and make money, she needed a business plan and some professional help. She was all alone here. How was she going to find the right people to set up the legal and financial aspects?

She took out paper and started to make a list of things she would have to do.

She felt she needed more of a security system, alert police and fire in an emergency.

She needed to install a pet door, so Unity could let herself out and not have to depend on Melinda.

Business cards had to be made in bulk

A designated phone and fax line needed to be installed.

Maps of the area needed to be available to people staying there showing points of interest. Most people had GPS, but sometimes a map was easier.

Insurance?

She needed to set up a bookkeeping system and a business account.

She was sure there must be county and state laws governing this type of business, so a lawyer was necessary.

People would need keys to the front door so that Melinda could run short errands or just take a nap!

The listing seemed to go on and on. It was a good thing that because this was a private house, she would dictate when and how many people could use the house at any given time. She could simply say that the place was already taken if she wished to vacation or have to leave town for some reason.

A strange twitch was attacking Melinda's neck. "Now what?" she said to no one in particular. Trying to dismiss the little electric-like sensation, she focused on other things.

Unity cuddled up against Melinda's leg. "You were a very good girl with all those people here." Melinda absentmindedly petted the dog. The effort was met with a soft sigh.

CHAPTER ELEVEN

Four years ago, James Carver, a 32-year-old convict, was sitting in his cell reading the local newspaper. James was a handsome man, about 6 feet tall, with an unusually good physique. He had a smile that could have been on a magazine cover, but he wasn't aware of his good looks. He did seem to attract women, though, but James had absolutely nothing to offer any of them. James almost considered jail his home; he was in and out of cells. Each sentence giving him a lengthier stay at the expense of the county. It wasn't that James was a bad person; he was just unfortunate. James was convinced that he never got a break. The rules for the outside world just didn't apply to him because he was a disadvantaged child that grew into a disadvantaged youth that turned him into a disadvantaged adult. Whenever he tried to get some of the "good" life, the rest of society just didn't want him to have it.

Poor James had been born to a 15-year-old unwed mother who abandoned him when he was barely two. He was raised by his maternal grandmother, who had all the love in the world to give him but lacked any way to provide him with materialistic things. Granny was one of those warm and wonderful people who just radiated love, but she was alone in the world except for him, and at the age of 59 and not in the best of health, she was not able to effectively handle such a small child. She did her best, though, and James now recalled that no matter what trouble he would get himself into, going home to Granny would be absolution and a sensation of safety. The home was two rooms that Granny occupied in a rundown house in a dangerous neighborhood. There were constant breakdowns in the tiny home, and James would try to repair anything as soon as he was old enough to make and handle a tool. Some of his repairs were ingenious, but no one except Granny knew about them. When James was 16, Granny passed on. James calmly packed a small bag of his possessions, kissed Granny on the cheek, said something he felt passed for prayer and left the house. He never came back to that location again. He knew that sooner or later, one of the church ladies would come looking in on Granny, and they would know how to take proper care of her body. That loss, coupled with his abject poverty, would set James on a path of self-destruction. James was not a malicious person; he justified all his crimes which were basically petty misdemeanors. He would reason that he took only what he really needed, that he would take only from people who had so much they wouldn't miss it, that the stores he would shoplift from were huge businesses that could easily take the hit.

Unfortunately for James, the stores, people, and society, in general, did not accept the way he was obtaining things. At the age of 32, he had a long, long arrest record.

The newspaper was just about the only thing James did read. He wasn't exactly illiterate, but his reading was about the third-grade level. An article caught his eye about a new church in Richmond. The simple statement about growth of spirit was a lot less prohibiting than other Church credo's he had seen. There were no threats, no time limits to save one soul, no hint of retribution. James decided to write to the address and see what would happen. He was hoping to get a handout from some do-gooder and their attempt to reform him from his evil ways. He was surprised when Charlene Adams walked into the jailhouse one day to visit. Charlene had no answers for James. He realized that she wasn't offering a handout or an easy fix for his life. Intrigued by her approach, James acted interested in whatever religious message she was peddling. He figured she was a woman of some substance, and he was going to play along with her and see what he could get out of it. She offered to come to visit with some written material that he could read in his own time and that she would discuss it with him and offer guidance. Figuring that with his looks, women were an easy mark and that he could charm some money out of her. His intention was to leave Richmond and head somewhere where he was less well-known to the police. In the meantime, claiming to have found religion would work well to extricate him from the jail cell.

Charlene kept her word and came twice a week to speak with James. They talked about everything, and James started to anticipate her visits. She offered him some advice, some possible solutions, and some spiritual guidance. Basically, she listened. Although James felt he was still scamming her, his curiosity was piqued. Religious Science was not a Bible-thumping, retributive religion. It was a philosophy of life, using one's own inner resources to deal with and solve everyday situations. Wisdom of the ages from all other religions, common sense and scientific method forms the core of the teaching. It's just that we are all Spiritual Beings having a human experience and that we could all tap into our divine heritage to strengthen our everyday lives. The readings were difficult; the language, though, was every day. With repetition and explanation, James was getting some of it, and it felt good.

Charlene had made some temporary arrangements for James upon his release. The recently acquired church building, which is very old and in need of many repairs, had a basement. Rooms were sectioned off but not currently in use. It was a half bath, and it was right off an area that was private enough to be a bedroom. On the main floor, the church has a small kitchen as well as some classrooms and two offices. The sanctuary was small, simple and totally unadorned. Only a piano and pews occupied this room. No altar, no religious symbols were there. A podium stood at the front, along with a long rectangular table.

James could live in the basement and use the kitchen as he needed. Charlene felt that the half bath, without a tub or shower, was the best she could arrange for now. James was looking forward to his new "home," already planning what he could take and how long he would stay in this safe house. He thought that perhaps there would be a collection box or safe. As his release date approached, James thought about how sad he would be to rip off Charlene. She was really nice to him, so attentive. He almost had a sense of Granny being with him. He shook off the sensation and reminded himself of who he was and what he was about.

CHAPTER TWELVE

The first guests of "Hickory Acres" had set a fire under Melinda. Of course, she realized that part of the success was due to the particular people that stayed at the house. After Thanksgiving dinner, the four guests, Ken and Charlene, had come back to the B&B and sat around the family room having a great time. They insisted that Melinda and Unity join them and for hours told stories, jokes and laughed till their sides hurt. Melinda offered wine and then was afraid that she shouldn't have. Not all ministers are allowed to drink! Her offer was accepted with an enthusiastic yes, and soon the bottles were uncorked and emptied and enjoyed. Ken had given Melinda his business card and wrote down the name of his accountant on the back. At that moment, she noticed that Ken was a lawyer. He said that the man was a financial genius, although a bit eccentric. The evening ended with Charlene and Ken saying goodnight to their buddies and making arrangements to get together again soon. Everybody knew that as much as they would like to, they had extremely busy calendars, and the likelihood of "soon" was a long shot. By midnight, the house was quiet. Melinda felt the energy of the people upstairs. She had heard them pray together before retiring, but the prayer was so different from anything she had heard before. It was purposeful and affirmative, no asking or beseeching. Melinda realized that she had only known these people for two days, but she felt as if they were her friends, not just her house guests.

She crawled into her bed, sad that the two couples will be departing in the morning. At that moment, she decided that she wanted some soda, got out of bed and went to the mini-fridge in her sitting room. A quick look revealed no soda, and with a sigh, she put on her slippers and walked to the kitchen to get some. Melinda had kept a night light in the kitchen just in case one of her guests needed something there. As she entered, the glow from the light reflected off the beautiful stone in the windowsill. It actually sparkled. She stood memorized for a minute or so, staring at the object. She approached the window and held the stone, turning it over in her hands. It was just a stone, but at times it seemed to take on a life all its own. She also realized that the needle-like sensation in her neck had disappeared. She chalked it up to anxiety over her first Bed and Breakfast adventure. "Tomorrow, I will start marketing myself!" Melinda thought of a way to get the word out that Hickory Acres was open for business.

Early in the morning, Melinda set out to bake dozens of muffins and cookies. By noon she had boxed them up and was ready to go and introduce herself to the community. She made a route to follow and made her first stop at the local firehouse. The firehouse consists of both professional and volunteer members. As Melinda drove up, she could see only a few people currently at the station; she geared herself up, took a deep breath and entered the station holding a couple of boxes.

"Hello," She said to a man sitting behind a computer.

He snapped his head to attention as he did not see or hear her enter.

"How can I help you?" Came a response as his gaze returned to the computer.

"Sorry to bother you, but I came to introduce myself. I just started a business nearby and thought you would like to sample some of the baked goods I make."

At the words "Baked goods," his attention came back to Melinda

"Oh, what have you got there? Hey John, come here. This is something for you!"

John appeared from another room and immediately eyed bakery boxes. As both men were fixated on the boxes, Melinda yanked them away.

"Hello," She said. "My name is Melinda, and you are?" A momentary embarrassment on the part of the men, and finally, they both looked at her.

"Sorry, Ma'am, we don't usually have visitors. I am Brian Williams, and this is John Hatcher. You said you are new to the community?"

"Hello Brian and John, yes, although it has been almost two years in the making. I have just opened up Hickory Acres. It's a tiny B&B. I do baking and catering, the catering only at my establishment, but the muffins and cookies can be ordered separately. I wanted to bring a sample, and I hope you enjoy it. I would really appreciate it if you could send someone to the B&B and check out any fire hazards you may see." Melinda extended the bakery boxes to the men. They eagerly snatched the boxes and grabbed something to eat.

John was the first to respond. "Oh man, this is delicious! Seriously, we could have some of these here every day." Brian seemed mesmerized by the chocolate chip cookies.

"You are a dangerous woman!" He said. "How can I tell my wife that these are superior to hers?"

Melinda was delighted. She left the boxes there, made an arrangement for the firefighters to come to Hickory Acres, and felt a boost of confidence in her ability to get this business going.

Her next stop, the police! Melinda realized she had never been to a police station in her life. Her contact with the police consisted of a few school incidents and a traffic stop! She had a terrible experience as the victim of a crime. Right now, she refused to let it cross her mind. In any event, her exposure in that incident really didn't involve the rank and file police. As she entered the building, located in a strip mall, she was sure this definitely wasn't like a NYC precinct. Melinda approached a uniformed young woman at the front desk. The name on her uniform was Melinda Clark.

"Hey Melinda, I am a Melinda too." The officer looked and smiled at the middle-aged woman in front of her.

"Hi, I don't get to meet many other Melinda's! How can I help you?"

"I am new to the community and just about to open my business; I wanted to introduce myself and bring some examples of the goodies I make. It's a small B&B with an on-premise catering and room for business gatherings as well as parties and weddings."

Melinda extended the bakery boxes, and officer Melinda's smile grew wider.

"Wait a minute, okay? Normally Captain Crenshaw does not like to be disturbed, but--- hey, this is different. What is your last name, please?"

Melinda provided the information, and officer Clark went to a rear office. With a box of cookies, Captain Henry Crenshaw looked up from his desk and immediately responded to the baked goods put in front of his face.

"Okay, send her back here. I will try to be nice."

Officer Clark answered him, "you'll be nice. You can't resist a cookie!"

She exited the office giggling and waved to Melinda to follow her to the rear office.

Henry Crenshaw was already standing up when she walked in. Whatever he was expecting, it was definitely not this attractive woman.

"Ma'am, he greeted her, already forgetting her name.

"Captain, " responded Melinda. "I hope I'm not interrupting anything important. I just wanted to introduce myself and give you a sample of the product."

She went on to tell him about the B&B and tempt him with the array of baked goods she made.

"I was hoping someone could visit my place to advise me on some security and who to call to have it installed."

Melinda knew she was being flirtatious. Captain Crenshaw responded similarly.

"Well, Ma'am, I would be happy to assist you. Where is your place located?"

Melinda told him the address. He knew it instantly.

"The old Wilson place! I knew they sold it, and I've watched the changes. Glad to know it's up and running. You caught me on a slow day. How about I go back to your B&B now with you?"

Melinda smiled and said, " Now that's service! That's great!"

Crenshaw had a spring in his step, and he ushered Melinda out of the office door.

"Clark," he bellowed, " I'll be about an hour. Going to the old Wilson Place."

Officer Clark smiled. Two things Crenshaw loved were baked goods and attractive women.

Henry Crenshaw had been to the Wilson place many times over the years. He was amazed at what it had become with the repurposing of the old farmhouse to a B&B with rooms ready to turn into a banquet hall and party room. He followed Melinda around the entire premises, all the while making notations. The two of them kept up the flirtatious banter. When the tour was over, they settled in the breakfast nook. They started to discuss the security that Henry felt was necessary.

The hour went by quickly. Melinda's head was spinning. Finally, Henry said he would call the security company and tell them exactly what he thought was needed. He looked at his watch and stood up to go.

" Melinda, there is much more I feel I should tell you, but we have to continue another time. How about this evening? Can I take you to dinner.? The smile on Melinda's face froze. The sudden shift was very noticeable to Henry.

Melinda said, " I don't do dates!"

"It's not a date, " countered Henry, " it's just dinner.!"

Melinda collected herself, " I'm sorry, I wasn't prepared for a dinner invitation. Dinner would be nice. Do you have a place in mind?"

"MMMM, I can tell from your accent that you're from up North, so how about a little Southern BBQ?"

"That would be great." She tried to keep her voice upbeat, but her discomfort was obvious to Henry.

"How about 6? I will pick you up. I promise you the food is really good."

"See you at 6." He hurried out of the house and to his car. He was disturbed at her strange reaction. His years as a cop told him that either she had something to hide or something had happened to her. Anyway, he hurried back to the station to make a few calls to see what he may uncover about Melinda Radnor.

CHAPTER THIRTEEN

Thanksgiving was the only American holiday that Aviva really celebrated. She thought about it for a moment, then figured no, there were two, Thanksgiving and the 4th of July. The other designated holidays in remembrance of Presidents, fallen heroes, etc., were just good reasons for sales and days off from school. The Yeshiva didn't follow the regular school calendar, but Thanksgiving was observed. Many in the community-made no special observance of the day for two reasons. First, they felt they gave thanks each and every day and didn't need a special day for it. Second, the holiday was based on the celebration of Christians. Aviva thought the rationale was ridiculous. Did those people think for a second that it was Christian because no Jews traveled on the Mayflower to experience that first hard and desperate year in the New World? Did "thanks" have to have a religion to identify it? She busied herself with the preparation of the turkey and potatoes. The mechanical movements freed her mind to think about the past few months and the direction her life had taken. She knew she was in a crisis and needed to get away from here and sort things out. The only place she knew to go was Virginia. She would call Melinda and see if it would be possible for her to come and stay a few days. She also knew she had to go soon. That would mean leaving school, but she didn't care. She knew it meant giving some explanation to her husband, and still, she didn't care. The only thing that bothered her was that her children would not understand and want clarification and she was not prepared to give it to them. Her children, although caught up in the tumult of their own lives, were well aware of their mother's unhappiness. Normally, Aviva was outgoing, bubbly, and full of questions. Recently she had become withdrawn and her complexion pale. Her daughter had even suggested she see a doctor because she feared her mother's changes were a result of illness. Aviva wanted to see a therapist but would not be able to explain why she would want to go out of the community when everyone knew there were perfectly good therapists right here who would "understand her better." Aviva feared that no one could understand her, or at least not condemn her.

While everyone was gathered in the living room after dinner and the dishes were in the "fleshadik" dishwasher, Aviva quietly went into her bedroom and dialed Melinda's number.

"Of course you can come here, and you stay as long as you need!" was the answer from Melinda to Aviva's question. The women made some tentative plans, Aviva would take the train from Manhattan to Richmond.

36

Melinda would be there to pick her up at the station. Aviva wanted to go tomorrow, on one of the busiest travel days of the year. Melinda assured her there were several trains that made the trip during the day, and she should just leave a message as to the time she was coming.

There was a problem of food, Aviva could only eat kosher, and Melinda did not have a kosher kitchen or even know if kosher meat was available in the area. Then she remembered the garage apartment with its own mini kitchen. Since it was never used, it would be appropriate for kosher use. One problem solved, the other would take some research, but until then, Aviva could survive on dairy and vegetable products.

Aviva wasn't sure how she should tell her husband of her plans to leave. The women discussed the matter and decided that it would be better to leave with Ari's knowledge, even though this may open up more discussion than Aviva wanted at this point. No need to complicate the situation with mystery. Aviva decided that she would tell Ari that night, that she just had to get away and that she was going to Melinda's. She also decided that he was not to call her and that she would contact him. She would tell him that her cell phone could be a point of contact in an emergency. She was leaving her return to New York open. She just didn't know how long she needed to clear her head. Finally, it was decided that Aviva would arrive on Sunday; this way, she would have Shabbos to break the news to her husband and children.

Melinda was shocked when she picked up Aviva at the station. She had never seen her this way, so sad and withdrawn. She had lost too much weight, and her eyes were red from crying. Her husband had not been understanding or supportive of her decision to leave. She resisted with all her strength to reveal the terrible dark secret for fear that he would do her physical harm. In the end, she just said she was leaving, and that was that! She would check in twice a day to see if there were messages on her cell phone; otherwise, it would be turned off. The parting words were angry and hurtful.

Melinda had tried to talk to Aviva but whatever it was that was bothering her was too painful for Aviva to discuss. Finally, Melinda approached her and said, " I think there is someone here in Richmond who can help you. But, you have to keep an open mind and trust me in this. She is a minister of something called Religious Science. I have no real idea what it is about, but my first guests here were all part of that religion. They were not only the nicest people, but they were open, nonjudgemental, and so spiritual. I have no idea if they are Christian or if they even follow the Bible. Still, there was something about them, and Charlene especially, that just earned my respect and gained my trust."

Aviva gave an emphatic YES because she was sure of one thing …..
They weren't Jewish! Somewhere in the recess of her mind Aviva
rationalized that if she could clear her conscience without Judaism, she
would be able to then face the consequences of her actions and resume
being a Jew. It was illogical for sure, but she just couldn't delve into the laws
and prohibitions and complicated maneuvers prescribed by her birth religion
to free her of her terrible guilt and continued desires.

With Aviva settled in her apartment, Melinda attended to business.
Charlene's husband, Ken, was a lawyer who specialized in business and
corporate matters. Melinda was his newest account.
She placed a call to the accountant that Ken had recommended.
Stan was working at his desk when the phone rang. "Wingate" was the only
thing he said. Melinda explained that she had received his name from Ken
Adams. She was trying to set up a business, and Ken recommended him
highly. Stan's mental Rolodex located Ken's name and made the association
of Ken's business and his wife's church. Melinda continued as to the type of
business she was about to embark upon and admitted that she didn't know
where to begin. She was hoping that she could make an appointment with
Stan and have him explain the steps she needed to take and what he would
charge for his services. She was more than willing to come into the city for
the meeting, but Stan thought he would be able to get a better feel for her
financial needs if he saw the place in person. An appointment was made.

CHAPTER FOURTEEN

When James had come out of prison and viewed his new home, he was very disappointed. It was quite frankly in poor shape. Not as bad as some of the places he had lived, but in definite need of repair. He could envision how things could be fixed and how improvements could be accomplished, but not too quickly or too cheaply. He looked around the entire building for several days and then approached Ken with his ideas for the repairs. Ken asked him what tools he would need, how much material would cost and how much help he would need for some of the larger jobs. James was very honest with what he thought he could do and what they needed a professional for. Ken then set out to obtain financing and materials for the repairs. It would stretch the little congregation to the breaking point, but everyone wanted to preserve their place of worship.

Projects had to be prioritized. The first huge expense was a new roof, and that, of course, was beyond Jame's ability to accomplish. But while the roofers were there, he kept a very close eye on the project. He spoke to a couple of the workers and asked them if they would like to help him with some of the smaller projects. They would be paid, but it would not be to the scale of their pay now. He convinced them it was good for their soul to help this poor struggling congregation. Whatever he said or promised them, they came to work in between their roofing jobs, and James became a foreman!

 In the meantime, James performed magic on the things he could do alone, and within a matter of months, everyone could see huge strides in the church facility. People in the congregation took notice, and before too long, they were asking him to come and take a look at projects at their homes. He was amazing; he could repair plumbing, electrical work, drywall, he could do painting and wallpapering. He could retile, he could fix floors, and he could do it all well and make it look fabulous. He got too busy! He knew the church came first, and everybody else just had to get in line. Although he could fix up his accommodations in the church, he decided to move to a nearby apartment that he could now pay for! He amazed himself that within a year, he went from the intention of staying at the church until he could figure out a scam and move on to a respected member of the community and a regular churchgoer as well. That nagging little voice in his head, always looking for a quick hit was diminished, but not gone.

James received a message on his cell phone (a perk from the church) from a woman named Melinda out in the suburbs. He had seen her at church occasionally, but he had never spoken with her. When he called her back, she explained that there were odd jobs she needed done to her home because she was opening up a B&B. After arranging a time to check things out, Melinda asked James if he liked cookies! As odd as that sounded to him, Melinda was very happy when he responded with an emphatic YES! Melinda said she needed an honest opinion about some cookies she had just baked, and he should come hungry. James had the use of the church van and headed out to "Hickory Acres" to take a look.

That old feeling crept into his mind, could he make a score here? He just couldn't help himself.

CHAPTER FIFTEEN

Charlene extended invitations to attend an informational meeting through newspaper ads and flyers. Her intention to come home to Richmond and establish this church was more difficult than anticipated. The church had grown, but very slowly. She never lost hope that she could grow the church to 400 members, with a teenage program, a children's program and babysitting for infants and toddlers so parents could attend a Sunday service. There was something that she felt was finally happening. She felt her goals were within reach and that her dreams would soon be realized. At first, she thought the appeal of this awesome, healing, teaching ministry would be for the unchurched, those without affiliation. However, she saw that there were many who attended church out of habit, not conviction. There were many who belonged to different congregations but felt unfulfilled and longed for a new approach to their spiritualism. Still, others had no idea what Religious Science had to offer, and Charlene was here to bring it to them.

Charlene had no idea how many would show up for her introduction to Religious Science. She decided to rent a room in a local High School and serve coffee and cake. Melinda volunteered to take care of the refreshments. She knew that she and Aviva would be attending the lecture. She wasn't sure what her motivation was for attending, but she wanted to check it out. Melinda was born Jewish but had no affiliation with any synagogue. She was known as a Holiday Jew, one who celebrates the holidays for family gatherings and food. Other than that, nothing. Aviva had no objection to the informational meeting because it was in a school. The idea of going to a church, any kind of church, was terrifying. Approximately 50 people showed up that night, Charlene was overjoyed. She absolutely glowed, and she stood in front of the crowd and gave the background and structure of the church. She explained that Ernest Holmes, in 1926, had put together a book after years of research incorporating the teachings of all the world's major faiths and the physical laws of the universe. He brought together different philosophies that all had the same universal goal. She told the crowd about demonstrations that have taken place using the power of the human mind and fueled by the presence of a Supreme Being, that which man refers to in different names such as Universal Mind or God. The tempo was upbeat, the people enthusiastic. Charlene concluded with some facts about the faith. "We have no rituals; we celebrate no special religious holidays, we are not governed by lists of shall and shall not. We simply learn to think for our individual selves, using the universal mind that creates our experiences exactly according to our beliefs. How many of you have said something similar to, every time I see so and so I get a headache, or I'll forget to take the tickets with me, or sooner or later I will get sick because it is flu season, and that particular experience happens! We are victims of our own thinking. We are so used to expressing things in the negative that we accept the consequences for our thoughts as mandatory. In Religious Science, we teach that by making negative statements into positives, we can create a whole new reality. I find so and so to be very stimulating; they always make me think.......I have tickets already in my purse, I am prepared, and therefore I won't forget, or I know what I need to know. I am always in perfect health. Now that doesn't mean we walk around with our heads buried in the sand, denying circumstances and situations in our midst. It means that we look for the positive to stop the situation from developing into problems by seeing them from a constructive point of view. As an example, if it's flu season, I tell myself that I know because I take care of my body by feeding it correctly, exercising and resting enough, my immune system is functioning properly to ward off the virus. In addition, through affirmative prayer, which we call treatment, I marshall my strength that comes from purposeful thought, which further strengthens me and protects me from ill-health. I can remember a time, about 30 years ago, before I found this marvelous teaching if someone approached me and said, "Oh Charlene, you look tired, and your voice sounds funny. Are you getting sick?" Even if I felt perfectly fine, by the evening, I would have a cold or laryngitis. I gave the idea of being sick the power to make my body sick. I realize this is an oversimplification, but I think most of you can relate to it.

Charlene spoke for another 15 minutes. Everybody walked away from the meeting with information they would need to digest. Melinda could definitely ask questions of health; others zeroed in on ideas of abundance and health of their financial affairs. The meeting was a total success, and it created curiosity about Religious Science. Aviva hung onto every word about guilt and anger. Charlene had people wanting to come back and hear more. The overriding message was that our birth religions taught us fear. Fear that if we stray from the regulations of our churches and temples, we are committing some grievous sins, and these sins were irreparable to our souls. Fear that if we don't give up the control of our clergy, we are doomed and fear that we lose God's love. This was a chance to see God in a new light. Melinda reflected on this, and the vision of that beautiful, strange stone came into her mind. "See things in a new light!" It was odd, but she felt a calmness and an inspiration take hold.

CHAPTER SIXTEEN

The weather was exceptionally warm in Richmond for December. In stores, Christmas carols were blaring, Christmas trees were being sold on numerous empty lots, and houses were wearing lighted decorations. Hickory Acres was an exception. It never crossed Melinda's mind to decorate for this holiday as it was not in her experience. Aviva had decided to stay with Melinda indefinitely. Each day, she felt the weight of her past actions become a little lighter. She just had no desire to return to her life and, most of all, to Ari. She made herself useful at the B&B, helping Melinda with the cleaning. Of course, no one had actually stayed there since the Thanksgiving weekend. Aviva's computer had been used less and less since she arrived. The compulsion to speak to strangers, male strangers, was passing, and Aviva was examining the reasons for her change of attitude. There were other attitudes that changed as well. She was feeling less suffocated by ritual. Although she still lit Shabbos candles, ate kosher food, and kept her head covered, she was feeling liberated.

Today, James and Stanford were both supposed to come to Hickory acres and make plans with Melinda for the financial and structural changes to the B&B. Melinda was trying out some new cookie recipes as she had plans to bake some presents to give those she had come to know here. As circumstance would have it, both men arrived at once. Stanford and his pristine automobile, and James in a rusty van with Religious Science written on the side. James had not yet felt comfortable enough to purchase a vehicle even though he could now afford it and had renewed his driver's license. As they entered the house and made their introductions to Aviva, Melinda followed with a platter of mouth-watering goodies. Unity came over to Stan first and gave a perfunctory wag of her tail, but when she sniffed at James, that tail started to wag at the speed of a hummingbird's wing in flight. The dog actually whelped with glee and turned over on her back to let James pet her belly.

"I have never seen her like that!" Melinda was almost jealous.

"Dog's love me." Came the answer from James.

Aviva watched Stan's face as he observed the adoring exchange between James and Unity. She noticed that his expression had not deviated from his entrance at the front door, as if he couldn't smile. She decided to end the moment by asking if anyone would like a hot or cold drink. James stood up from his position with the dog, and Stan came back into the moment and answered, "yes, I would appreciate some tea, please." The four people and Unity made their way to the breakfast area through the dining room and took seats around the kitchen table.

Melinda had prepared a list for James, which included everything from a doggie door operated by a device in Unity's collar to additional lighting along the driveway.

Stanford had prepared forms, figures, facts about the start-up costs and presented it all in a neat package. He had included tax information as well as a bookkeeping setup to be considered. Melinda felt overwhelmed. She looked up and saw that Aviva understood perfectly what Stan was saying. In that split second, Melinda knew she had a business partner. It was a perfect division of labor.

Melinda excused herself and took James on a tour of the premises, leaving Aviva and Stan alone to finish the discussion. Stan made a remark about a chess game, and Aviva lit up with an enormous smile.

"Do you play chess?" Aviva inquired

"I play very well, but I lack competition here. Do you play?" Stan still hadn't changed expression.

"I too think I play very well," came the response from Aviva. "Perhaps we can play one day soon."

Stan was suspicious of the invitation. He was not accustomed to people asking him to participate in a social activity. He was also sure that this woman couldn't possibly be a proper opponent for him. This was the one area where he felt invincible. He studied the petite woman sitting next to him. She was quite attractive, but there was something foreign about her. Was she wearing a wig? Did she have some kind of illness that made her hair fall out? What kind of a name is Aviva?

"I think you are afraid of the challenge." Aviva chided.
That did it; Stan didn't want to back down from this. "Okay, I accept the challenge, but be prepared to lose and to lose quickly."

Aviva laughed at the attitude. Stan almost cracked a smile in reaction to her delightful laugh.
James and Melinda returned from the house tour. James had the information he needed and told Melinda that he would write up an estimate. Before the men departed, Melinda had them rank the cookie selection and then gave each man a bunch of his favorite.

CHAPTER SEVENTEEN

Aviva made an appointment to speak with Charlene. Aviva was so anxious that she couldn't relax even in the comfortable atmosphere of Charlene's study. Charlene started talking, " I am not a psychologist. I know that you have some secret that weighs very heavily upon you. I think you have come to me because you are seeking some kind of absolution for whatever it is that you did, that you perceive to be so horrendous. Before you tell me anything, I want you to know that I cannot give you absolution. I can only guide you as to how to forgive yourself. If you feel that this isn't enough, or this isn't what you want, then I suggest that you see either a Rabbi or a psychologist."

Aviva was not expecting this; she supposed on some level that she was seeking absolution, even if it wasn't through her own tradition.

" Is what I say to you totally confidential?" Inquired Aviva.

"Yes, nothing that is said in here goes further. Let me ask you, why did you come to me, why not someone of your own faith?"

"What I did was horrible, and I didn't want anyone who knew my family or me to look at me with hate." Aviva couldn't control the tremor in her voice.

"Who did you kill?" questioned Charlene.

"Kill? I didn't kill anyone!" was the outraged answer from Aviva.

"Of course not," Charlene smiled, "but that is what you are comparing it to in your mind." Charlene continued, " Before you tell me what it is you think you did, let me explain. Religions are based upon divine input. People, especially those living 5,700 years ago, for example, had to develop societies to preserve their populations. They were divinely inspired to make rules and regulations to control every aspect of the people's lives to keep them from harm and to keep them together. Some of these rules were common sense, some ridiculous, and some had reasons that we still don't understand. Just as the species of humans keeps evolving, our religious ideas evolve as well. What happens in all dogmatic religions is that the word of God gets all mixed up in the stories and writings of man. Therefore in one religion, it becomes sinful to dance, while in another, it is a virtue. God, being all that there is, has given us the ability to continually grow with free will. Whatever we do in our lives is a product of the speck of divine spirit within us and decisions we make formed with our thoughts and intellect. This spirit allows our thoughts to manifest our realities. Whatever your reality, if you wish to change it, then first trust in the divine spirit and then change the thought to change the behavior. Now, if you wish, tell me what has you so tied up in knots."

Charlene sat back in her chair to listen. Aviva made the decision to go ahead and spill her guts to this woman who she hardly knew but instinctively trusted.

"I have committed the sin of adultery. I had an affair with a man who I met through the internet." Aviva just blurted this out.

"And…" prompted Charlene.

"And? Isn't that enough?" cried Aviva.

"Enough of what? In order for you, a married woman in your tradition, who practices all the religious rituals even to the point of covering your hair and using a ritual bath on cessation of menses, must have overriding reasons to have slept with another man!"

As the conversation progressed, Aviva told the whole story. She was drowning in desires. She was craving attention and affection. What she got were financial support and materialistic things. She had made attempts to communicate her desires, her concerns but always met with a stone wall of silence. To her, it was a form of abuse. Aviva told Charlene that she was married at nineteen and conceived very quickly thanks to the laws regarding sexual intercourse. She never took any fertility drugs but had triplets naturally. It took her quite a while to get back her strength and stamina after the birth of the children. After that, Ari, her husband, was nervous about subsequent pregnancies. She also felt that she had three, and that was enough. They spoke of birth control, agreed upon a method, but the threat of possibly conceiving again made her husband distant. In time, that extended to all forms of affection, and no matter what she did or said, they grew more distant until finally, she felt little for him at all. Then there was the sex itself.

Ari was her total experience with sex. She had never thought it was such a big deal; it was tolerable at best. She wanted the play, the pre-sexual activity. This is what she found, first in the banter with Eagle and then in the bed. What started for her as a rejuvenation exploded into a thrilling, physical experience. She craved him more and more until the mental aspect of her behavior, the guilt, started to erode the physical pleasure. Now, all she had was a memory and an intense desire to have more and an enormous guilt that she had given into the desire in the first place.

She listened and then asked, "Did you and this man use protection against pregnancy and VD?"

"Yes, always," answered Aviva.

"Okay, so you are sure there is no possibility of pregnancy or sexually transmitted disease."

"I am 100 % sure," answered Aviva

"All right, with that concern out of the way, see if you can accept this. I know it to be the truth that you are a spiritual being having a human experience. As a human, you are subject to desires and needs. That is a scientific fact. Some of these needs are physical, others mental. We know as an example that babies fail to thrive and often die if they are not held and cuddled. Even if they are fed, kept clean, and are safe, without the loving, they perish. Yes, there are exceptions, some may go on living, but they never recover to be what is considered normal. As adults, we all still need affection and love. We can find this love inside ourselves, and that can sustain us. When we are living in a society where we are paired up in couples, we expect the affection and love to come not only from ourselves but also from our partners. You had a need, there was a lack and limitation in your experience, and you did something about it to fill you up. Your husband is not a bad man; he was just incapable, for whatever reason, to give you that which you so badly needed. You found that you were living in a vacuum and not knowing how else to handle it. You had the tool of the computer to create that which you needed. You were only doing what was necessary for you. Forgive yourself. Admit to yourself that your behavior was predicated upon a lack in your life. There's no irreparable harm. God does not judge; people judge. All God ever says is yes, it is up to us to handle things as well as we can. If you are distraught over the incident, then change the thought that created it to happen. Perhaps you should consider divorce. What is the sense in living with someone who cannot fulfill your needs and instead drives you to another? In all likelihood, Ari will not change, and that will cause this to happen again and again, or you will choose to be miserable by living with him. You have options. Listen to the spirit within, that little voice that knows the answers.

About an hour later, after more talk back and forth, Aviva returned to Hickory Acres and locked herself in her apartment. Melinda knew that she was home but figured that Aviva would come into the main house when she was good and ready.

All night Aviva thought about Charlene's words and about her own religious convictions. She cried, she hit pillows, she ate ice cream, and by the morning, she concluded that she did indeed want a divorce from Ari, and if he refused to do this amicably, then she would tell him about her affair. She also knew she didn't want to return to New York but wanted to speak to Melinda about remaining here indefinitely and that she was going to go to a local Rabbi and see where his guidance led her. She felt that her traditions and faith were so much a part of her life that she just couldn't give them up. She also knew that she was going to take a good long hard look at her Orthodoxy and what those teachings have said to her, and perhaps there would be some changes ahead for that too.

47

CHAPTER EIGHTEEN

Slowly the word got out about the lady at the B&B who baked the most marvelous muffins and cookies. The fire department and the police were now regular customers, and Melinda discounted boxes going to the stations greatly. Orders started rolling in from individual firefighters and cops. Melinda's goodies had been part of everyone's holiday festivities. At the B&B, many of the recommendations from both fire and police had been installed, and Captain Henry was a frequent visitor. He had tried to research Melinda and even made some calls. There was definitely something there, but the information was classified and sealed. He couldn't imagine what she had gotten herself into. While she remained flirtatious, she kept her distance, much to Henry's chagrin. He showed up one evening at the B&B to announce his retirement. After 25 years on the force, he had enough. He made the decision to go to Florida. He had two brothers there, and they owned a horse farm. Since he had grown up with horses, he was looking forward to dealing with equine problems instead of human ones. He would be staying on a little while longer in the area. He wanted Melinda to know that if she needed anything, she could still call on him during his transition of preparing a new Captain in his soon-to-be-vacated position. He also told her that she could always count on Officer Clark for anything she might need.

The new year had arrived on the wings of mild weather and gorgeous winter sunsets. It seemed as if the whole city was just waiting for a snowfall that was reluctant to appear. Snow in Richmond is usually a yearly event that only leaves a few inches and quickly melts away. Occasionally, a good dumping of six inches or more cripples the city totally. Melinda laughed that the supermarkets would be jammed with the hint of snow in the forecast, while schools will close with the threat of snow and stayed closed till some imperceptible all-clear was sounded. This being so different from her teaching days in New York, where it would practically take an ACT OF GOD to simply close the schools for a single day.

Many changes had to come to Melinda and Hickory Acres. In the last few weeks, James had transformed the master bedroom suite into a little fortress. An alarm system had been installed per his directions to isolate the sitting room and sleeping area from the rest of the house. This way, Melinda could feel safe from the clientele if she felt the need. There was no screening process in a B&B, so this effort was deemed necessary. The door leading to the enclosed porch was fitted with a doggie door that worked on a sonic system with the control to raise and lower the opening in Unity's collar. From there, a swinging doggy door let Unity exit from the porch to the yard. It took the dog less than a day to use it. When Melinda wished, she could simply turn off the transponder in the collar to keep the door closed. A visible barrier would show the dog that the door was not available for use. James had also sectioned off the third car stall in the garage, under Aviva's apartment, to create a cedar-lined store storage area. Now that the upstairs bedrooms were reserved for guests, Melinda felt that she needed some personal storage space. With this alteration, she can store files as well as clothes. The guest rooms were all hooked up to smoke detectors, as well as the hallway between the rooms. These sent signals directly to the fire department and the security service. The quarters above the garage space were also alarmed for safety. Aviva would have plenty of storage room in the cedar closet for the clothes she will be receiving soon from her New York home.

Melinda wasn't feeling well again. Her stomach was bothering her, and she never knew when it would react to food or situations. At times she felt like a prisoner in the house because she was afraid to travel too far from her bathrooms. She had been diagnosed with IBS, irritable bowel syndrome, many years ago. In fact, the doctor had done a fluoroscopy and had actually seen her colon spasm. Other symptoms plagued her, and she knew that with her knowledge and use of the internet, she could drive herself crazy thinking she had a slew of fatal or at least debilitating diseases. She would feel the panic rise, further aggravating her stomach and ending in a red flush along her face. Even though she tried her best to ignore it, she couldn't stop the progression of the upward spiral of discomfort into anxiety. She had started reading the principles and practices of Charlene's church, and her talks with Charlene were helping to keep her sane. Melinda had started to take some quiet time each morning to meditate and then to say a small prayer called spiritual mind treatment. She had started to attend, when she could, the weekly meeting at the church and always walked away feeling better for the effort. She kept saying to herself, over and over, change the thought, and you change the behavior, but starting this business was a huge undertaking, and she wanted everything to be perfect.

Truthfully, she didn't doubt her ability to make Hickory Acres a success. Still, insecurities from childhood made her nervous about starting it and not being able to keep up with it in the event that it becomes successful. Different cliches such as, "you always bite off more than you can chew," ran through her mind, in first her mother's and then her husband's voice. Was she really capable of this undertaking? Her children thought she was loony. "Why would a woman of your age start such a demanding business when you could take it easy?", "What are you going to do if you get sick?", "Mom, you are always sick. Can you handle this?" These were some of the concerns voiced by the two of them. In the meantime, her worried offspring didn't feel it imperative even to come and visit with their mother and her new home and location. Not even the promised Christmas vacation time came to be.

CHAPTER NINETEEN

After much soul-searching, Aviva realized that she wanted a divorce from Ari. The only way to tell him was in person. It took all her courage to come back to her home in New York for this purpose. Ari was not a particularly easy man to talk to. Aviva had prepared a statement to read to Ari because she knew that she would waver in her resolve to tell him outright of what she wanted. When they settled down for a big "talk," she withdrew the paper and read in a shaky voice.

"Ari, I know that you and I have been together for many years and that we have both worked to make a happy home for our children. I think that as parents, we have done a very good job and that we have raised three strong people who are now able to be out on their own. You know that over these past years, I have not been happy and not fulfilled. We have grown farther apart from one another, and know that our obligation as parents has changed, I want to go and explore who I am for myself. You have provided me with a nice home, but the distance between us emotionally is more than I can handle. I know that I can't change you, only myself, and I have come to the conclusion that I want out of this marriage. I must tell you that I am only asking your permission to grant me a divorce and not that I am asking your permission to leave. No matter what you decide, I am gone. I would just hope that you make it as easy for both of us as possible. I want to take with me only what is mine. I can work and make my own money, but I want what I have already earned on my own. I hope you understand."
Ari sat stunned. When he spoke, his voice took on a menacing quality that Aviva never heard.

"You ask me to let you go? What about me, what will people say? I have a place in this community; I have a position that others look up to. Now you ask me to show a weakness, that I am not a good husband? Do you realize that you are not the only one that is not too happy? What is happy? You think you are 18 perhaps and that you will find love and excitement? We all settle, we keep up appearances, we make do. What will the children say? What do I tell everyone? You are a selfish woman."

Ari sat silent for a moment. The quiet was overwhelming; when he finally spoke again, it was like thunder.

"I will give you your divorce. I will let you take what was yours, and that's all. I will not be drained of my hard-earned money, and I want you out of here tomorrow. I never want to see you again, but I realize because of the children, there will be times when that will happen. I know this is the work of that woman. See, I warned you, you become friends with the goyim, and they change you from a good frum woman to a whore!"

Aviva was shocked. He knew so little about Melinda, and he didn't even realize that she was born Jewish. Aviva decided not to correct him. But a whore? The word hurt, but to scream about it would bring up the affair, and she wanted to avoid that at all costs.

Due to the laws of the state, the final decree for divorce would take quite a while, but as long as both parties were in agreement to divorce, the religious bonds of marriage could be dissolved instantaneously. Aviva would return to New York just long enough to appear in front of a religious tribunal to have the "get" issued and claim the marriage over. She packed up her things, mainly her clothes and personal items, and left the address to have them sent. Any other property that Ari and the children decided not to claim as their own would be sent to her at a later date. She knew this would not be her last trip back to New York, but when she left, she felt the weight of all those years of misery lift off her.

To save face, Ari told everyone that Aviva had a mental breakdown and would be away from home recovering. He figured that in time, he could come up with some story to explain her extended absence instead of the fact that they had been divorced. He had tried to figure out exactly what happened. He thought he had everything worked out. He never once considered that Aviva wasn't an extension of him but an independent, intelligent woman who needed more than what he provided.

Aviva had started that promised game of chess with Stan, and to his surprise, she really knew the game! He was not able to defeat her easily. In fact, he couldn't defeat her at all. The chess game had continued for quite a time now. It was tax season, and Stan was occupied with business. Aviva had to settle for little bunches of time to make a play in this very serious tournament. The two of them had come to respect and like each other. Stan had relaxed and actually smiled frequently when in Vivi's company. He had nicknamed her because he just couldn't seem to be comfortable saying the whole name with a Southern drawl. Aviva had ceased to wear the "sheitel" or wig that first caused Stan to regard her with suspicion. Her own hair was lovely. A rich auburn that enhanced her natural good looks and seemed to match her pretty eyes. It was an educational process for both of these people. Coming from such different backgrounds and ideologies, everything that came up in conversation was an awakening to new ideas and customs. Both of them were enjoying the discovery.

CHAPTER TWENTY

The Bed and Breakfast was now ready to make the official opening. Some guests had stayed for a night or two since the first trial way back in November. It was similar to a practice run. Now, the grand opening was to take place, and the house and grounds looked marvelous. All the county business was in order, advertising had been placed in magazines and online, and a grand opening celebration with all friends in the Richmond area and Charlene's Atlanta cronies about to take place May 1st. Melinda and Vivi had been busy for weeks baking goodies. The interior of the house was Spring cleaned and was spotless. James had come to inspect all the carpentry, plumbing, and electrical work just to be sure everything was in 200% working order. James didn't do gardening, even though he probably could. Just not his thing. Hendricks, the gardener, had all the bushes and trees trimmed and a sea of spring flowers spread out in full bloom surrounding the driveway and house front. A small garden had been added along the rear of the house against the screened porch area. Lawn tables and chairs were placed along the tree line, and Melinda thought it was the prettiest sight she had ever seen.

Melinda had received responses from 35 people, including her children, that they would be there for the opening festivities. When she allowed herself the time to think about it, she would cramp up and spend the next few hours in and out of the bathroom. She had come a long way and now stopped herself from the negative thoughts that had always permeated her mental chatter. Still, she was having difficulty quieting that subconscious stream that would overwhelm her and send her into stomach spasms. When the feelings of impending doom would overtake her, she would now be able to calm herself down and know that she was centered in the present and that there were no threats in reality to hurt her.   Unity understood that something big was going on in the house. For the most part, that sweet, beautiful dog would acknowledge the arrival of people at the B&B and then retreat to some spot in the room where she could keep an eye on Melinda and the action. At night, Unity kept her place at Melinda's side. No matter how hard Melinda would try to keep the dog off the bed, Unity had the idea that it was HER bed. Every morning, Melinda had a bed partner. Unity seemed to approve of everyone but had an odd reaction to the gardener. A low throaty growl, barely perceptible, would emanate from the dog. Melinda had a request from the man to keep the dog away from him. It seems he had a bad history with dogs, and no love was lost between them. Melinda assumed that Unity could just feel the vibes from this guy and that he was not a dog lover. Odd how that always seems to happen. The person who is afraid of the dog is the one that the dog seems to single out. She knew from personal experience that if a cat were in the area, it would find her lap because she didn't particularly like cats.

James was most definitely Unity's favorite person next to Melinda. Each and every time that James would come to Hickory Acres, Unity would greet him like a long-lost lover.

With just a couple of days left before the grand opening, Vivi, Charlene, and Melinda decided to have a girl's night. The weather was glorious. Richmond had awakened to Spring in such a lovely way. The air was fragrant with blossoms and the temperature comfortable, everything in glorious shades of greens, yellows and pinks. With the windows open and the ceiling fans whirling, the three women settled into the family room after a delicious dinner at a local restaurant. Sharing a bottle of wine and knowing that three flavors of decadent ice cream were waiting in the freezer, the women relaxed and started talking about that past. The conversation flowed easily even though the subject turned to topics that previously would have been taboo to them.

"Sex is overrated," declared Melinda.

"Maybe in your experience," countered Charlene with a wink. Vivi offered that she couldn't say with certainty if it was good or not. She decided that good sex was a combination of your partner and your motivation.

"Was it ever good for you, Melinda?" asked Vivi.

Melinda looked at her two good friends and decided to tell them about her past.

"Do you two really want to hear details of my sex life? It may shock the hell out of you", said Melinda.

The two women, both a little tipsy, perked up and sat straighter on the couches.

"OHHH, you have a past? Giggled Charlene.

"Seriously, yes, I have a past," offered Melinda.

"You never said anything to me at all. I thought you didn't date after your divorce. You never mentioned any other men.

Vivi felt like she had been cheated out of Melinda's confidence.

"From where you were coming from, I didn't think you would be interested in my sex life, and I knew that you would be judgmental, and I didn't want any of the guilt stuff from you.

Vivi knew she was right. "Yes, of course," she answered. I guess I was a real pain in the ass."

The other two women laughed to hear Aviva use language like "pain in the ass!"

"Okay," said Melinda. " This is both painful and difficult for me to tell. After my divorce, I felt ugly, undesirable and worthless. I decided that I needed to get out into the world and attract another husband. I felt incomplete being by myself, and I felt incapable of raising the kids alone even though I had financial support from Michael and I had my own income as well. I didn't know any single men. I had been so cloistered in my little social circle. Friends had offered to set me up on dates, but I would have rather kissed a frog than go out with some of the guys they had in mind. I felt the only way to meet someone attractive and exciting would be to try and be interested in hot sex and frequent places that would attract men. I had the time to do it. The kids spent every other week with Michael. I delved into sporting events, horse racing, and dancing. I dressed provocatively and put on the persona of a femme fatale. I learned quickly that if you set your mind to it and had a little creativity, you can send out vibrations that say, hey, I am sexy, and I want you! It wasn't difficult then to attract men. I had more invitations than I could handle. Unfortunately, I sent out the vibes that simply said, "here I am, fuck me!"

Vivi absolutely winced at this last pronouncement. Melinda continued "Now, I am a realist, and I know that I am not gorgeous, but not ugly either, just an average-looking woman. You would have thought that I was a Playboy bunny. Sending out a message is only half the game so, if you put it out there, you have to keep up your end of the promise and come through the sex. I would say 98% of the men I met couldn't care less about me, my personality, or whether I was a mass murderer. Just as long as they could stick their penis into an orifice, and it didn't matter much which one. I was careful, but on occasion, I would slip up, and some guy would ejaculate somewhere in or on me and find amusement in my discomfort. Every now and then, there would be a genuinely concerned man who wanted a little more from a relationship and would be caring. I was a girl who just knew her husband and what I would consider acceptable sex. I didn't have any experimentation as a kid, but I became very educated and very quickly. I probably could have been quite a high-priced hooker if I had chosen to be. No sexual practice was off-limits except things that inflicted pain. I refused, although I was asked several times to either be a slave to someone or dominatrix. I could have won an Academy Award for my performances. I could make men who were terrible lovers think they had made me achieve the orgasm of the century. For all the sex, all the adventures, I was bored and no closer to finding husband number two. It took some time to realize that sex was overrated, and didn't want any more of that scene.

There are places you can't imagine, parties with lavish accouterments as well as filthy motel rooms, where people spend hours and hours of their time weekly just screwing everything and anyone who is willing. There were

56

nights I would stumble home so sore from multiple partners that I thought I would never recover. There were days when I doubted my sanity for my behavior. After coming back from a" weekend" party that made me so sore it was painful to urinate or defecate, I decided that vaginal and anal sex were out. For the next few months, I was the blowjob queen. I perfected the art of oral sex. I think I could have made a fortune at that too. This went on for quite a number of years.

Then, one night sitting in a posh Park Avenue apartment, I looked around at all the glassy-eyed, insincere, sexually addicted, slightly, to extremely perverted specimens of manhood that felt that they were better than everyone else because of their money, and I got sick. Sick to my stomach and sick of my life. I didn't say goodbye after puking my guts up in the swanky bathroom; I just walked out the door. I changed my phone number and had it unlisted. I sent an email to those people I wanted to continue to hear from, telling them about a change in my email address and screen name, and I never looked back. I didn't date for a year, and then not too often. I know that the problems that sent me through that route in my life were not resolved. I am sure that my constant illnesses and conditions are all resultant from the same causes that made that period of my life possible. I didn't ruin anyone's life, and luckily for me, after that episode, there were no lasting effects. The sex queen is dead; long live Melinda, the B&B princess. Melinda ended her story here. Melinda knew she was still not telling the whole truth. That was something she thought she would stay silent about for the rest of her life. She was still not able to tell the finale to anyone.

"Here, here," Charlene cheered.

Vivi had listened to the exchange in stunned silence and then burst into peals of laughter. "And I thought I was bad. I can't believe it! Everything I ever wanted to know about sex, and all I had to do was ask my girlfriend!"

The night wore on, the bottle of wine finished and quite a dent made in the three tubs of ice cream. The women talked and revealed many past secrets. They spoke of hopes for the future and felt a camaraderie that was unparalleled in their individual histories. Their paths had led them to this place at this time. There was no doubt that this was simply the way it was meant to be. Three women who had journeyed from three different points to come together and experience the one truth, as expressed through the one mind and made manifest in each of their own uniqueness.

CHAPTER TWENTY-ONE

Hickory Acres was off and running. Not only did the reputation of the lovely rooms and grounds circulate through Richmond, but the talents of Melinda's wonderful breakfasts and dinner parties. The phone would ring off the hook requesting information on the rates to stay for special weekends. There were requests for weddings on the premises as well as group outings from the local civic association and Social Clubs. Melinda had to turn away so many because she booked up the B&B 4 months in advance. Vivi, as she was now known to everyone, took care of the financial aspect of the B&B and helped Melinda with the preparation of the larger dinners. Two local women were hired to help with laundering sheets and towels as well as cleaning the house and preparing guest suites for occupancy. Melinda would oversee all the preparations and invariably go over everything before the guests arrived. Since most of the action was limited to weekends, Vivi and Melinda would use the weekdays to plan, shop, and unwind. Sometimes, a local group would request a party or dinner at the B&B and just use the lower level. Melinda was busy all the time, and she was so very happy.

Over several months, Vivi and Stan spent all available time together, and it was obvious that there was more than a chess game in their minds. A tremendous change had come over Stanford Wingate III. He had learned how to smile frequently and participate in conversation. In fact, sometimes it was the most garrulous of all. He developed a sense of humor and seemed much more at ease with himself.

One quiet evening the two women were having dinner when Vivi decided to confide something to Melinda.

" Stan is a virgin!" Vivi blurted out.

Melinda, mid-swallow, almost choked on the pronouncement. Not that she had expected anything else, but was just so surprised to hear it come out this way from Vivi.

"And how did you find this out?" Melinda asked as she recovered.

"Every time we get a little affectionate, he backs off, and finally, I just came right out and asked him if he was gay. I assumed that a man of his age would be clear about his sexual orientation. He was so flustered at my remark; I don't think he ever even thought about it. He said he knew he wasn't gay but probably asexual. I decided to put it to the test. He was easy to arouse, but he stopped himself, dead in his tracks, went into a shell and confessed his ignorance because he had never been with a woman. I couldn't have been more clear that here was his opportunity! Then I realized how severe his insecurities actually are. Now, I have a mission."

Melinda was hysterical. "My friend, the sex therapist."

Vivi was offended by Melinda's howls of laughter. "NO, I'm serious about this. Stan needs me, and it's the first time that I feel that I am really needed by another except for being a mother. I am going to save this man from living his whole entire life without experiencing love and sex too!"

Melinda calmed down and looked at Vivi. "Honey, I don't want you to be hurt. He may not be able to give you what you want from him. I think it's amazing that he has come this far in such a short time. I realize this is all your effort, and it is admirable but is he a project, or do you really have feelings for him?"

Vivi considered Melinda's words.

That evening the phone rang, and Melinda answered in her most businesslike voice. "Good evening, Hickory Acres. May I help you?"

"Mom?" asked the voice of Dianna, Melinda's daughter.

"Dianna, hi!" Melinda always enjoyed hearing from her oldest child.

"Mom, I have some bad news, Daddy had a massive heart attack, and it doesn't look good."

Melinda took a moment to register the news. Her ex-husband, Michael, the father of her children, had had little contact with her over many years. They were cordial when they had to interact, he was very supportive with money, but on a personal level, he was always distant. Michael had married and divorced twice more since his marriage to Melinda. She automatically wondered where his two ex-wives were.

"He is asking for you, Mom," Dianna added.

Melinda thought better than to inquire as to the whereabouts of the second and third Mrs. Radnor.

"What hospital is he in?" she questioned.

"North Shore, he is in the CCU. Daniel and I are here with him, but he keeps asking if you will come. Mom, do you think you can?" Dianna was close to tears.

"It will take me a long time to get there. I'll see if someone else can come with me because I hate to make a drive that long by myself. I'll be there by morning, one way or another."

Mother and daughter spoke for a few more minutes and then hung up. Melinda turned towards Vivi and asked her if she could possibly make the trip with her. Within an hour, all was decided. James was able and willing to come out to the B&B and stay with Unity. He had no other responsibilities but the dog's care since there were no guests or functions scheduled for the next week. He assured Melinda that he would take perfect messages and that he "wouldn't mess the house up too much." Vivi contacted Stan to say that she would be out of town, and then the two women packed a little suitcase with a couple of changes of clothes and toiletries. The drive would take about 6 hours at this time of night. They would go directly to the hospital and then worry about a motel room after Melinda saw and spoke to her children and her ex-husband.

CHAPTER TWENTY-TWO

Stanford Wingate replaced the receiver on the phone and smiled as he thought about the woman who had just been on the other end. "Vivi," he said out loud. She had come into his life and gave him a whole new outlook on its existence. They had begun a chess game, and in spite of his initial superior attitude, he found her to be a formidable opponent. Whenever they could manage to find some time to play that first game that delightfully went on forever, he realized that he was smiling. Her ease, sense of humor, and intelligence won him over. He was reluctant to engage in conversation at first, afraid that she would shut him out and... and.... he didn't know. He was just afraid. She kept coming back, though, and each exposure to her made him bolder and eager to see her again and again. He knew that she was still legally married and that she was running from years of a bad experience. He knew that she had three grown children that she loved and grieved that she was separated from them. He knew too that she was searching for more meaning and depth in her life. What he never expected was that she could find fulfillment with him! As they played that game, they would talk more and more. Little by little, they would go out and walk or stroll through the city or take in a movie. Stanford was not too interested in eating, so Vivi's dietary obligations were never a problem for him. She would prepare a meal for the two of them, or they would frequent the restaurant where she could find appropriate food for her to eat.

It was the increasing intimacy that had Stan worried. From the earliest age, he could recall tuning out on any conversation that dealt with sex. He was so convinced that his appearance was appalling that he didn't allow himself any hope of making love to a woman. He never considered any homosexual activity either. This was totally distasteful to him. He occasionally would engage in masturbation, but his learned code of ethics made this a disgusting activity. He felt weak and belittled after he would relieve himself. It was easier to bury deep inside any fantasy of sex or any desire to feel sexual.

He was petrified at Vivi's desire for him. How could such a beautiful, wonderful woman want him? What could she possibly see there that would cause her, no, compel her to share herself with him? He had slipped a couple of times. He had gotten an erection as she whispered in his ear and gently touched him. He would concentrate with all his strength to tune her out and think of something ugly to make the temptation go away. He knew that she would not stop, and God help him he really didn't want her to. He also knew that if he kept up that kind of behavior, he would eventually cause her to go away. Then he would be safe, but at what cost? He wished he had someone to talk to, a buddy, a brother, but there was no one.

He remembered an incident in his life. It was insignificant and should have been forgotten as soon as it happened, but it had stuck with him. He had gone to a fair at the church. There were all kinds of booths and games and food. There was a little stage with some magicians and a comedian. Little Stan had taken the seat in the front row of the audience as the comedian came onto the stage. The jokes were off-color. Stan, about ten years old, didn't understand any of them. The audience, however, was roaring, and Stan thought he'd better laugh too, or the comedian would be insulted. Stan laughed the loudest. The man on stage pointed at him and said for everyone to hear, "Hey, what are you, a midget? You, short guy, you understand what I'm saying?"

That sent the audience into laughter once again. Stan was devastated. He ran from the stage area straight home. He spent the next few hours in his bedroom staring at himself in the mirror.

"Maybe I am a midget. Maybe I will never be any taller? Maybe my mother is right, and I will never be good for anything." He came up with so many reasons why he was inferior to the whole world that he believed it. He looked up famous midgets and again felt he could do nothing right because he was too tall to be one. He fell into no category, just short. It would haunt him forever. It would extend to every area of his life, save one, and that was his work. In his work, Stan felt he was a giant. It was solitary work. Once people gave him the facts and figures to work with, he would quietly and efficiently get busy.

Now, with Vivi in his life, he was starting to question if there was more. More for him, more than the bottom line, more to that growing craving that he tried so hard to dismiss. Perhaps there was even more to Stanford Wingate than anyone had ever thought.

"Vivi," he said out loud again. "You strange and wonderful woman, do I dare and let you in?"

Stan thought back to everything he had ever heard about "those people." Oh yes, of course, he had dealt with Jews in business. Richmond had a sizable Jewish population. They had been people, just like any other group. He had never known any, though on a personal basis. His mother was not fond of Jews. She took an attitude that Jews were like bees that would pollinate the summer flowers. They were there, they were necessary, but they were unwanted. If only they could do their business, then go someplace else, out of her sight and out of her social circles. At best, one can say she was tolerant, acknowledging their right to exist. It was just a case of "not in my neighborhood."

62

A large grin broke out on Stan's face as he pictured introducing Vivi to his mother. Too bad Mother was in no mental condition to appreciate the irony.

Vivi had explained to Stan some of the reasons why she did things in certain ways or why she had covered her hair when they first met. She had told him of her struggle to understand her own behavior and how she was reconciling her relationship with God. She had told Stan that before she came to Richmond, she did things in a certain way because she was told that it was sinful to deviate from rigid teachings. She had thought that she was well educated, but she never asked the really hard questions and, being a woman, felt it was not her right to object to the way things were "supposed to be." When she broke away, she started to view the world and her religion differently. With the help of Charlene to point out where the rules and thought patterns that created the rules emerged from, she felt liberated to explore her religion and believe in its values for what they were. Inherently good and sound practices had come under the control and or interpretation of some who, for various reasons, had manipulated the initial divine message and perverted that message to suit their own needs. It was not dissimilar to mob psychology that whipped up people's emotions into a frenzy and made them capable of behavior that individually they would not have participated in. More recently, Stan could see this happening in the Muslim world, where a peaceful, loving message of the prophet Mohammed was twisted to promote war and mayhem.

Stan had so long ago stopped thinking about any emotional issue that the world opening up to him was like a floodgate. The emotions, the thoughts, the sensations were rushing in at a pace that was uncomfortable and at times incomprehensible. If Vivi had found peace and was experiencing joy from Religious Science, then maybe there was something for him there too? Stan decided to attend one, maybe two Sunday morning services to see what it was all about. "hmmm," he thought, " another thing to bring Vivi and me closer."

"Okay," Stan proclaimed to no one but himself. The next time they were alone, and the mood was obvious, he would try just to let it happen. What exactly "it" was, he wasn't sure.

CHAPTER TWENTY-THREE

Michael Radnor lay in the hospital bed hooked up to various machines that whined and beeped and hissed. The tubes going in and out of various parts of his body, plus the somber lighting in the cubicle he occupied in the CCU, made Melinda recoil. She collected herself and approached his bed. Gently taking his hand, Melinda saw his eyelids flutter open. He was not able to talk because of a tube down his throat, but he could signal yes or no to the questions by squeezing the hand of the interrogator.

She smiled and said, " Gee, you look like hell! " What could only pass as a smile flashed over Michael's face. Normally a handsome man, Melinda could see that he had lost weight and had a gray haze to his complexion. Lines were deeply etched into his face.

He took a pad and pencil and wrote back a message. "Hi beautiful, good to see you too."

Melinda smiled. "I hate to see you like this, Mikey." She was the only one to have ever called him that. "The children are concerned. You do have intentions of walking out of here, don't you?"

Michael wrote back. "It looks kind of bad. Don't think I am going to make it."

Melinda, not missing a beat, yelled out, "Bullshit! You love a good fight, and we aren't finished yet. Give me a couple of minutes, and I know I can think of at least ten things we haven't ironed out."

Michael wasn't surprised at her spirit. He knew she was strong, stronger than she herself had known, but she was so much more than the passive girl he had married. Melinda had finally come into her own, and he was proud of her. Sadness clouded his eyes; he thought maybe if he hadn't been such an insensitive prick, he could have stayed with her all these years and wouldn't have made the same mistakes over and over with two other women.

Melinda continued talking, "you have one thing to do right now. I want you to concentrate on your strength, think that you are well and whole. I know that you will leave this hospital under your own power and that with some medical treatment and some rest, you will recover fully. I mean it, Radnor, believe it, and you are well. This is a temporary setback."

Michael scribbled a note, "I asked you to come to take care of my final wishes. I need to know that everything is in order and that the kids are taken care of. Be careful." Melinda read it and answered. "Okay, I will promise to take care of the final wishes of Michael Radnor when the time comes, but now isn't the time. Someday you and I will die, but it isn't today, and it's not tomorrow or in the foreseeable future. I don't know if you can understand this, but I just KNOW you will be fine."

Melinda reached down inside her and believed, not just wished, but believed that Michael was fine. It was already taking place, he was healing, and he would come back from this setback no matter how major it seemed to be at this moment.

Michael needed to sleep; he wrote that he would try and be more positive and that it just made him feel better that she was there to handle things should that be necessary. She bent over and kissed his forehead and told him she would be back later in the day.

When Melinda came out of the CCU, she faced the worried and nervous faces of her children. "Let's get some breakfast. Dad is resting, and there is nothing we can do for him by standing here."

Daniel, and Dianna and Mom, along with Vivi, left the hospital and went to a nearby diner.

Diners were one of the few luxuries that Melinda really missed about NY. It amazed her that this type of establishment just never caught on outside of the tri-state NY area and, of course, Florida, where the number of New Yorkers had mushroomed over the last 25 years.

She sat down in the booth with the others and studied the enormous menu. Finalizing her decision, she closed her eyes and tried to sort out her next move.

"Okay, " she began. "Your father has hit bottom, but he will bounce back. I don't want any what-ifs! We take one day at a time. He is in a crisis situation right now, and the best thing we can do for him is stay calm and not feed into any negative attitudes. If we have to deal with something different later, we will handle it then. Right now, I can stay for a couple of days, but then I have to go back. Anyone have anything to say?

Daniel looked at his mother and smiled." When did you develop such a take-charge attitude?

Melinda looked at her son, then at Vivi and Dianna and realized that she had taken charge and she was fine!" Nothing hurt, nothing felt wrong, and all of a sudden, she felt euphoric." I guess I am just growing up. It takes some of us a lot longer than others."

The rest of the breakfast time went along smoothly, filled with conversation. Melinda told the kids to go and get some rest. Maybe we could go to the motel and get a room. Dianna and Daniel could take a room, too, since the ride into Manhattan would take too long. By the time they got to Dianna's apartment, they would have to turn around and come back. Melinda would take the first turn at the hospital. The visiting hours were very limited, but she was sure that Michael would know that she was there. Vivi took advantage of being in New York to call her children and try to see them in the next day or so before she would return to Virginia. The doctors had made an evaluation of Michael's condition. It was a consensus of opinion that due to blockages in the main arteries to the heart, surgical bypass was necessary, and the operation was to be performed immediately. In spite of Michael's sedentary and stressful lifestyle, he was in fairly good physical shape. Blessed with a cast-iron stomach and fabulous metabolism, Michael had never really watched his diet or thought about regular exercise. He had figured that he just wasn't prone to that middle-aged spread and that cholesterol and all the other baddies of the cardiac world couldn't harm him. Perhaps he was right, but the stress and strain of his job and the type A personality did catch up with him, and here he was on his way to the OR.

The entire family, and Vivi, returned to sit with Melinda in the hospital. With all the papers signed and all the encouraging words said, he was wheeled away. Melinda placed a call to Charlene. They did a spiritual mind treatment, which is an affirmative prayer and Charlene assured her that everyone back at home was thinking of her. Vivi took out her Siddur, or prayer book and recited a prayer for the sick. Dianna and Daniel prayed in whatever way they knew how and felt comfortable. They all waited.

The waiting seemed interminable, but in the end, the doctor came out and spoke with the family. Michael was okay. The next 24 hours were critical. The surgery itself went well, but now it was just a matter of time. As the hours ticked away, Melinda spoke with her children and told them about her life in Virginia and how well the business seemed to be going. She was so enthusiastic about her B & B and so happy with her accomplishments. She told them of her friends and the Religious Science Community. Daniel laughed and said it was a cult, but he had to admit, this was Mom as he never before saw her. Both he and his sister had heard of Vivi in years past, or Aviva as she was known then. They had even seen her a couple of times, but they were aware of huge changes in her too and understood that both women seem to have a new lease on life.

Daniel told his mother about his work, his girlfriend and soon-to-be fiance, Sarah. He was settling down at age 35. Sarah had been married once before, straight out of college. For whatever reasons, the marriage didn't last more than two years, and Sarah now thinks it was a question of maturity for both she and her ex-husband. Sarah was a dentist, happy in her work and ready to move on in her own personal life. Daniel said he had been waiting to give her an engagement ring before calling Melinda to let her know what was going on. Sarah was quite a bit younger than Daniel, and at first, he was a little concerned about the age difference, but they had worked it out.

Dianna told Melinda that she and Scott, her husband of four years, we're doing just great. She told her how much they had loved visiting the B&B for the grand opening.   Most of all, they had an announcement to make! With a little luck, a baby, a grandchild, for Melinda would make an appearance in about six months! Whoops of Joy came out of Melinda's mouth. "Why didn't you say something to me sooner?" Melinda questioned.

"I was just waiting to get through to the 3rd month. I didn't want any disappointments. Now, it seems silly to wait. I know that Dad would like to know too, " said Dianna.

"Gee, Mom, I will be 36 when the baby is born. You were a mother with two kids ages 10 and 13 by then!"

"Times and circumstances are different, and we are different people. Look at all you have accomplished to make you a complete person. You will be a terrific Mom, and you won't ever have the insecurities that I did. I am so happy for the two of you I could burst!" Melinda's voice had climbed an octave.

The next two days passed, and it seemed amazing how well Michael was doing. The tube down his throat had been removed, and he was able to talk.

"Mikey, I must be getting back to Virginia," Melinda told him on the morning of her third day in New York.

"Why, Mel, can't you stay a little longer?" Michael almost sounded frightened.

"I have things to look after, and there is the business." She explained.

" Stay longer Mel, that isn't a real job." He countered.
 Melinda thought twice about screaming at him. Here he was, lying in bed after thinking that he was at death's door and already he was negating her life.

"Darling, you are a very important person, and to some people, so am I. However, you choose to view what I do is not important. I have responsibilities, and I want to get back to them. You are in good hands here. You will rally. I hope that after you recuperate, you take some time to re-evaluate your schedule and attitude. If you need me, you know where I am." Melinda wished that the last conversation with him before she left would have had a different tone. Still, Michael was in the same place as he was before, while she had moved on very, very far.

Before she and Vivi said goodbye for the trip down I-95, the family discussed coming to Richmond for more than a quick visit. It was time to meet Sarah, it was time to get excited about the baby, and it was time for them just to be together. Both son and daughter promised that they would coordinate their schedules and give Melinda two or three separate weeks so she could clear the calendar to hang out with her kids. The surprise for all of them would be that Michael was coming. He thought it would be a great place to get his strength back.

CHAPTER TWENTY-FOUR

James loved being in the big house. Unity loved having James there too. He decided to occupy Melinda's bedroom. He studied just how she arranged the bed so that he could change the linens and remake the bed perfectly to prevent her from knowing that he was staying there. Arrangements had been vague. He realized that Melinda's departure hadn't been planned. Therefore nothing definite had been decided about the living arrangements when she was gone. He promised to take care of the dog and the property, and he was doing that in grand style. He roamed through the house, taking in all the art and knick-knacks. He looked through books on shelves and through Melinda's personal items in her dresser and in the bathroom. He felt as long as he didn't take anything or disturb anything, he wasn't doing anything wrong. It was amazing to him that the consciousness of his youth was still there with him. He no longer gave in to it, and he could quickly pull his mind out of it, but that voice of the child was there. Unity didn't seem to mind his investigation of the property at all. She would look at him as if he were a long-lost lover. It was an unusual reaction, for although Unity was generally good with most people, there were some that she found objectionable. A few times, when guests arrived at Hickory Acres, Unity would release a low growl from the throat. Melinda would interpret this as a sign that a particular guest had to be watched. It was the same negative reaction to Hendricks, the gardener.

Hendricks was busy at the house from the end of March through the start of December. With a long driveway, the garden beds, the dead leaves from the many trees, there was always something to take care of. Unity would let that low growl out of her throat with the approach of Hendricks' truck. Melinda would have to bar the doggie door and isolate Unity in the sitting-bedroom area. Hendricks did his job, didn't say much and had never set foot inside the house. All conversation about the garden and lawn took place outside. Melinda had hired him immediately after settling in the house. She had seen his truck across the street and approached him. He looked at the job and set his price. The trouble was that he kept raising the price and then would back down a few dollars at Melinda's protest.

James walked outside and surveyed the garden walk. Hendricks did a satisfactory job. Actually, Hendricks had arrived to do some work while James was house-sitting. James approached him, and the two men exchanged some words. James identified himself as the B&B caretaker, a title he had bestowed upon himself. Hendrix was surprised to see a black man at the house acting like he owned it. For some reason, it angered him.

Melinda called James to inform him that she would be returning the next day. That morning, James stripped the bed, took the linens and towels he had used to the laundry room and ran the machines. He prepared himself a large breakfast of bacon and eggs and coffee and toast. He cleaned the dishes, remade the bed, folded the towels and put them in the linen closet. He inspected the bathroom to make sure it was spic and span and then told Unity how much he enjoyed her company. Like a love-sick teenager, Unity just panted and cooed.

James left a note for Melinda saying that all was well and that he was glad she was coming home. There was a list of telephone calls that had to be answered, and the mail was piled neatly on the kitchen counter. There was a bill from Hendricks for trimming and fertilizing or some such thing. James thought that it was the wrong time of the year for those services, but he admitted he didn't know enough about gardening to be sure. He set the bedroom security alarm, placed Unity inside with her doggie door access available and vacated the premises. He felt that he had a little vacation as he drove the short distance back to the city and to his apartment.

CHAPTER TWENTY-FIVE

Upon her return from New York, Vivi decided to surprise Stan. She didn't call, but she let herself into his apartment with the key he had given her. She left a huge note so that he couldn't miss it by the front door. She wanted to surprise the man, not shock him. The note said, "if you want it, come and get it!" As it got close to the time of his return, Vivi changed into a sexy negligee that she had been keeping just for the occasion.

Stan had had a busy long day. His mind was full of figures and files as he made his way home. He was grateful for the walk to clear his head from the swimming numbers. It had been one particular account that just didn't jive, and he was concerned as he couldn't find the error for hours. Finally, the missing piece of the puzzle was located, and the numbers made sense. His head hurt, but as he walked, his thoughts turned to Vivi. When was she coming back? Did she say? He entered his apartment and immediately felt her presence. The inviting note quickened his pulse. The headache made itself known again. There was music playing in the bedroom.

"Vivi?" he called.

There was no answer. He went into the powder room directly to wash his hands and relieve himself and then took a deep breath before entering the bedroom. Before him, sprawled across the bed, was Vivi in scanty lingerie. She had a huge smile and delighted in the expression on Stan's face. Stan became frozen in place. Vivi hadn't quite expected that. She rose from the bed, " Stan, do you find me attractive?" She asked in a throaty voice. Finding his tongue, Stan answered that she was the most beautiful woman in the world.

"Stan, then come here and show me how beautiful I am to you."
He wanted to move but found that his feet had become rooted to the spot. Vivi, feeling frustrated but not showing it, started to take off his clothes. First, she loosened his tie and removed it next to the jacket. She started at the buckle of his belt. All the while, he just stood there as if unable to move a muscle. She unbuttoned his shirt and told him that she wanted to make love to him, but her words went unheard. She opened his pants and started to slide them down, and that seemed to be the switch that sent the electricity through his body.

" I don't know what to do, " he stammered.

" Don't think about it. Just do whatever you want. It's all here for you. If you want, don't do anything at all, and I will do it all."

She led him to the bed and put him gently down, enabling her to remove his shoes, socks and pants legs. His mind suddenly thought about how clean his underwear might be. It didn't matter, for Vivi had it off in seconds. Here he was stark naked, on the bed, with this woman who really wanted him. Before he could register any other thought, Vivi started to remove the negligee and began to caress and massage his body. The sensation of arousal began in his groin, and Stanford Wingate III needed no other encouragement.

There was a first time for everything, and this was the first of many. This time Vivi had been the teacher, the seducer. This time was different from those with her husband too. With Ari, her initial sexual encounters were nervous and not too pleasant. Eventually, it became almost pleasurable, but before long, it became rote and then just flat. With her lover, her encounters with Eagle, the nervousness gave way immediately to exhilaration, the physical sensation just fabulous, but the mental aspect was anguish. With Stan, there was no nervousness, no expectation, just the desire to please him, knowing that, in turn, she would be pleased. Although clumsy initially, instinct took over and together with Vivi's encouragement and guidance, the experience was blissful. Vivi knew in her heart that Stan was her soul mate. On the surface, they were so different, worlds apart actually, but she had identified within him some secret that only she could see. He was not good-looking, not bad looking either, he was short, and that would seem to bother him more than anyone else. He was socially stunted but finally coming out of his shell. He was for Vivi, the man who would cherish her and she was for him, the savior of his solitary and meaningless life.

CHAPTER TWENTY-SIX

Three weeks after coronary bypass surgery, Melinda had a house full of family. Dianna and Scott stayed in one room upstairs, Daniel and Sarah in another. Michael was doing so very well but insisted on occupying the master first floor bedroom. Melinda didn't even flinch with this arrangement. She knew that sleeping next to someone and in a huge bed was not the same as sleeping with someone. Melinda was not going to be thrown out of her own room. Unity was much more perturbed. She issued that low growl when Michael arrived and continued to regard him cautiously. Michael kept asking Melinda to " put the dog somewhere." Melinda would do no such thing. "This is more the dog"s house than yours, "was the response.

Vivi had decided to spend the week with Stan at his apartment so that the family could be alone.

Sarah was delightful. She fit right into the camaraderie between her two children and Scott. Daniel had finally given her the ring as soon as he returned to his Connecticut home. Dianna liked her immediately when she met her on the ride down to Virginia. Dianna was feeling a little queasy these days. With her trim figure, only those who knew her very well were able to discern that she was pregnant.

The weather outside was glorious. Early summer is delightful in Richmond. The only drawback is the proliferation of pollen, all sorts but especially from trees. Every morning the cars left outside of the garages would be covered in a thick coating of green. Melinda would be sneezing her head off a year ago, but for some reason, she was tolerating this allergy season well. She reasoned that her happiness and personal growth were helping to control her physical reactions. She realized how much of her past had been mind over matter.

The whole family was impressed with the beauty of the house, the way it was decorated and by the lovely location. Melinda was already famous for her baking and cooking, and everyone was excited to partake of the goodies. The surprise was that she had really developed a business. The phone calls requesting information and booking reservations were numerous. The calendar was filled with confirmed appointments. Michael looked through her calendar and started to find ways for her to expand her services and increase her cash flow. She stopped him cold, explaining that she was doing exactly what she wanted to do and that the purpose of this B&B was to keep her happy but not to work herself to death. Michael made several more attempts to explain the economics of business. Finally, Melinda looked at him and said, " Michael, this is my house, I answer to no one, and I like it like that. If you keep budding into my business, you will have to leave."

Michael was amused by her tone, so he continued with, "I was only making suggestions."

"Thank you, but no thanks. If I want your input, I will ask for it."

"Way to go, Mom!" shouted Dianna.

Actually, it was Dianna that was most impressed by Hickory Acres. Not just the way it looked and operated, but by the way, it made her mother so happy! The two of them had a quiet moment alone in the kitchen. Dianna picked up the unusual stone from the window sill.

" Mom, what is this?" asked Dianna.

"Isn't it pretty? I found it walking through the woods beyond my property when I was first settling in. I was intrigued by the coloring and shape. Ever since I picked it up, I thought of it as a good luck charm, and it has had a place on the sill since."

"You know, Mom, I never gave it much thought, but now that I am having a baby, I realize just what a terrific job you did with Daniel and me. It must have been hard for you with Dad being difficult and then not being around."

"Oh Dianna, that is one of the nicest things ever said to me. Thank you, you and Danny are my best memories of all those years, and I am thankful to have had you two." Melinda had tears well up in her eyes. "Mom, I want you to think about something. This is totally up to you and I don't want you to feel any pressure, OK?" Dianna raised this question, "Scott and I have been talking seriously, even before we came here about making a major change. We didn't know what we were considering just that we looked at Dad and what his work and his attitude had done to him. Scott wants to be part of his kid's lives and with the pressure of New York and the lifestyle we have, he just knows that he wouldn't be there for them. He'd probably end up like Dad with a heart condition. I realized too that my work schedule would have to be compromised unless I want someone else to raise my kids. That's why I look at you and marvel at how you did it all. Mom, what I am trying to ask is that Scott and I really love it here. We think it would be a much better environment for children and Scott's work doesn't depend on location. He travels a great deal of the time anyway, and if we stayed in New York I would be alone a lot. What I'm trying to say, Mom, is we are thinking about moving here, somewhere near you."

Melinda was so shocked she didn't know how to answer.

Dianna continued, " We could sell our condo easily, the market up there is great right now, and we could rent a place until we find something right. I could either look for something part time or help out here."

73

Melinda didn't think for more than a second, "I would love having you two here, I mean you three! How super for me that I get to be a part of a grandchild's life! YES!"

Dianna and Melinda had huge grins on their faces and hugged each other. Life is about changes, and what a pleasant change this would be, planning for a wedding, watching Dianna grow bigger with the baby tucked safely within her, Scott and Dianna making plans for a move to Richmond, and who knows what else. Somewhere in the back of Melinda's mind, she knew to enjoy the moment for truly that is all you ever have. In the famous words of the poet Henry Wadsworth Longfellow, "trust no future however pleasant." For now, Melinda took the stone on the windowsill and said softly to it for no reason at all, "Watch over my house and family."

During the week, Michael took a walk each day, he would start out of the house, down the driveway and follow the perimeter of the property. He would end his walk back at the driveway and walk back up to the front door. Each day he would add a little speed to his walk. He was feeling great, just a little nagging ache by the incision line. He was also feeling bored and jittery. It was so quiet here. How can anyone stand that much quiet? Michael realized he didn't know how to relax, but a steady diet of this would be torture. He was still working, answering a million questions on his cell phone. His office was never out of reach and he had his secretary jumping all the time. He questioned Dianna and Scott's decision to leave the Big Apple and settle here. Did they realize what they were giving up? Although Melinda had told him that New York was not the only place in the world with theater, music, and restaurants, he reminded her that the number of choices here was so very limited. To Melinda this was part of the charm. She felt she could always go to DC or NY for that matter if there was something she really wanted to see that just wasn't available here in Richmond. Michael couldn't understand why anyone would want to leave the excitement of the Big Apple unless they were broke or a hundred years old.

After a full week, Dianna, Scott, Daniel and Sarah had to get back to their lives. With lots of hugs and kisses they departed knowing that all of them would be together soon for all the festivities. Only Michael decided to stay on longer, he convinced work that he still needed the recuperation time although he had been doing business from his phone for almost six hours a day.

Michael also met Hendricks several times actually, as he would drive his truck onto the driveway and make himself look busy.

"Mel, that man is ripping you off. He hardly does anything but keeps writing you bills for services rendered."

"I know," Melinda was aware of Hendricks' scheme. " I keep track of his bills, and when it gets to be too much, I talk to him about it. The man is doing his best and I would hate to fire him, he really needs every job he can get."

"That's you, Miss Do-gooder." Michael scoffed at her charitable attitude.

 Nevertheless, on his own, Michael confronted Hendricks. He told the man in no uncertain terms that he better stop screwing around with the made-up bills and just do the job he was hired for. He threatened him saying that Melinda may be the lady of the house, but he was the money source and it would dry up quickly if there was any more of this bullshit. Hendricks didn't like the tone or the message. He was resentful that Melinda, that other woman, the black guy and now this one seemed to have so much when he had so little and they all felt like they could tell them what to do and how much to charge for it. His anger was growing and he was going to let off steam one of these days. He waited for an opportunity to get Melinda alone and complain about all this abuse. Melinda listened, and then started to laugh. " Mr. Hendricks, she finally said, " This is my house, I hired you and if necessary I will fire you, but no one, and I mean no one has the right to tell you what to do. I am sure Vivi has never said anything negative to you, it is not in her makeup, I am sure that James was just feeling a little cocky because he was staying here while I had to run to NY, but most of all I apologize for my ex husband who is a prick. He has no place to speak to you at all; he has no say whatsoever in running this place. I love what you have done here, and I would recommend you to others. Sometimes you pad the bill a little, but it's like a game. How about I add some of the baked goods to each month's bill and we just keep the price the same". Hendricks thought about it for a second or two, and then said that he liked chocolate.

Unity went wild on the days that both Michael and Hendricks were at Hickory Acres. The dog would start with the low growl and then just stare at them. If one of them got too close, she would bear her teeth and give the impression of being vicious. Melinda had watched this with amusement. This was the dog you could approach and take a bone out of her mouth without fear of being bitten. This was the dog that would come looking for comfort and protection from thunder.

Besides hating the dog, Michael started to find fault with many things. He would say something gentle such as, " You know Mel, you can have a larger TV screen in the family room." Then after she would ignore him he would get more obvious. He saw fit to criticize everything from Melinda's breakfast to the decor. He told Melinda that this house was a white elephant and that when she would get tired of playing B&B she would have a hard time dumping the place. "What do you need this headache for?" he would

75

comment. He became annoyed with the way she did his laundry and revived an old argument between them about the proper way to handle his shirts from the dryer. She found herself screaming. "If you don't like the results do it yourself!" He never did try it on his own, he just liked to yell at her.

He would go on and on not even realizing that everything coming out of his mouth put her down or humiliated her efforts. He was most vocal about her affiliation with Religious Science. " Those people are just bloodsuckers. Can't you see they are money-grabbing bible-thumping jerks? Did you lose your mind when you came here? I can't believe you would get involved in any kind of organized religion!"

"Michael," she started," I can see you still don't have a clue how to be a human being. I am sorry you can't appreciate the wonderful things that have happened to me or realize that I am truly happy. I thought for a minute there, with you in the hospital bed, that you had learned a lesson. The world does not revolve solely around you. You obviously don't have all the answers. I have found something that works for me and that I understand and agree with. I like what I am doing and I am not thinking about selling or stopping the B&B. If the time comes to end this, then I will deal with it then. I will not worry about what may or may not be. I love it here and I love what I have created. It is mine, it has nothing to do with you. If it does not reflect your taste, then too bad. I think it is time for you to leave. As we knew many years ago, we can't live together, and furthermore, I don't want to live with you. You are forever a part of me but we need to keep a distance between us. You are welcome to come and visit but in the future you have a choice of one of the guest rooms or go to another hotel. We are going to be grandparents Michael. Your grandchild will be down here. I'm sure you will want to make an occasional appearance. I love you, but I can't live with you."

Michael made arrangements to leave the next day. Melinda was thrilled to have her peace and quiet, and complete bedroom back. Unity approved this arrangement.

Michael wasted no time when he got back to New York. He started to investigate James and Hendricks and compiled a list of complaints against each man. He was ecstatic uncovering James' criminal past and the many harassment charges leveled against Hendricks. Without the knowledge of Melinda, or anyone else, he started to write letters to the local authorities about the "criminal" incidents he had witnessed at the B&B. Although he was not the owner of the property, he felt it was his duty to protect the woman who owned and operated it because she was too naive to see the problem. He did not write it all at once, but sent several letters over a period of weeks. He tried to convince himself that he was doing this all for

76

Melinda, but deep down he really knew that he was pissed that she had it under control and she was happy.

James, Hendricks and Melinda had no idea any of this was taking place and things just continued normally. They did notice however that there were more frequent patrols of police. Nobody really thought much about it.

Captain Crenshaw was fully aware of the letters and accusations arriving from Michael. He had Clark keep all things related to the B&B in a separate file. He had regularly kept in touch with Melinda and was a frequent visitor to the premises. At first Henry really thought there was a chance for something to happen between him and Melinda. They just were at different places in their lives and trying to woo her away from her beloved B&B was never going to happen.

Henry had just a little time left before he was officially retired. He would be relocating to Florida to spend time with his brothers who owned a horse farm in the Sarasota area. As pleasant as that sounded to him, he knew Melinda Radnor would never be happy there. They just remained friends which suited Melinda very well.

CHAPTER TWENTY-SEVEN

Summer in Richmond is not unlike New York summers. It gets too hot and very humid. It must have been the muggiest day on the calendar when Dianna and Scott made the big move. Scott had given his company his notification of transfer to Richmond. It was up to the head of the office to either reject or accept his choice of location. Had Scott been your average mid-level management employee, it would have been a foregone conclusion that he would be out looking for a new job. Scott was, however, an asset to his company and it didn't hurt that he had the right social and economic background to play right into the corporate mentality. He was aware that his parents had a great deal to do in paving the way for his career and he was thankful. He also knew that favors go so far and the fact that he kept his employment was due to his hard work and dedication. Scott was aiming high and he knew beyond a shadow of a doubt that he would rank in top management in the not-too-distant future.

Dianna would have the option to be a stay-at-home mom, or she could work part-time and eventually resume a full-time schedule. Right now, she was not making any decisions because she had the luxury not to.

The apartment they took was only minutes away from Melinda. The plan was to stay there for a few months, up to a year if necessary until they could locate the house of their dreams. Melinda was only too happy to help Dianna look for the perfect place to live.

Summer proved to be slow for the B&B. It seemed that Richmond was not particularly a summer destination for travelers. On most days, Melinda could understand why.

Daniel and Sarah had planned an October wedding. Deciding where to marry was a problem, now his Mom and Sister were in Richmond, his Dad in NY and he was in Connecticut. Sarah was not too keen on a big wedding, as this was her second. Daniel, on the other hand, wanted a big party to show off his bride to the world. A compromise was made. There would be a quiet ceremony in Connecticut with all the closest people to Sarah and some of Daniel's friends and then a second ceremony and gala in Virginia at the B&B. Anyone who wanted to attend the first ceremony would be more than welcome, but at least this way, people from the North who couldn't attend the party, for whatever reason, would still be able to witness the nuptials. Everyone seemed satisfied with the arrangements. This would be the only time that Melinda would hire a caterer in her own establishment. She wanted to be a guest at her son's wedding. Michael would be returning too. This time he wouldn't occupy Melinda's bedroom. She would make sure of that.

It started insidiously just a little cold, some scratchy throat sensations, nose, a little runny. Melinda was surprised, she hadn't had a cold all winter and now in the height of the summer the sniffles! She had first felt it in her armpit. An uncomfortable fullness but chalked it up to irritation from shaving. A few days later along with the cold she noticed the swelling at the base of her neck, not a lymph node, no detectable mass, just a swelling that was slightly sore to the touch. Melinda started to " treat" that she was whole and healthy. She practiced her affirmations and took care of herself nutritionally. If for some reason her immune system was compromised, she would nip it in the bud and be back to normal. She was sure that it was just a fleeting thing.

The nagging intestinal problem seemed to flare. It got to a point where she was afraid to leave the house because she never knew when her bowels would kick in. Again, she sat down to meditate and "treat" for the problem but she couldn't begin to figure out what mental process was at work. Nothing seemed to fit. Which thoughts were creating her reality? She stopped to consider the wedding, the baby, the presence of Dianna in Richmond, at anger and resentment. They were always there in the past, but she thought she had dealt with all that and that it was behind her. Whatever was nagging at her remained a mystery.

Melinda convinced herself that she was too busy to be ill. Most of the time she did a fine job of keeping the worry on the back burner, it was just when symptoms arose or worsened that she would feel the old panic set in. She decided to see a doctor, although which one was a question. She didn't want to involve anyone else in the process. That night, lying in her bed with her nose stuffed and whistling with each exhale, she reached with her left hand to scratch an itch under her right breast. They're up towards the chest wall and the armpit she discovered a small lump. She could feel the flushing of her face and then immediately had a nauseous sensation in the pit of my stomach. Her brain frantically thinking about how long ago was her last mammogram." My God," she exclaimed, "I am totally falling apart." She just knew that she couldn't handle this alone any longer. She wasn't sure where to turn for support.

One of the most difficult situations is finding a doctor in the city where you were new. Of course there are many who are competent, but do they take your insurance, are they experts in any particular field, do they communicate well with their patients, do they prescribe a lot of unnecessary medicines? The list goes on and on. Melinda called Charlene for a recommendation. Right there, was a huge difference in the habits of the two women.

Melinda had always believed that when given a diagnosis, it was up to the patient to research everything available to make choices about her own health care. While it was admirable that she was a participant in her own recovery process, the lack of sound medical background often led her to make erroneous conclusions.

Charlene's experience had shown her that once a diagnosis was given the best course of action was to" treat" on a spiritual level and trust in the expertise and knowledge of the physician who was scientifically trained and divinely inspired to help cure the patient. A diagnosis to Charlene meant just a possibility of an outcome, not a statement of absolute. She had known too many cases where the diagnosis was rescinded after spiritual mind treatment.

Charlene definitely believed in the use of physicians and the marvelous developments and strides in the medical world. She felt that once you and the doctor make a decision about the course of treatment, leave the medical aspect up to the professional. The patient must then work on the problem from a mental point of view knowing that whatever has created that reality is a false idea and not supported by the universal mind. Together the mental work and the physical work would yield the best possible healing. Melinda decided that her old method of panic, fear, and escalating pain had not gotten her too far in the past. She would take the recommendation, see the doctor and treat for the solution to the problem. She made an appointment.

There was a vast difference between her Doctor's office in NY , and the one she went to in VA. Of course, because they didn't know her they had to go over her TOTAL history. She had to send for her records from the old office, which she was afraid was more like a book. She had kept with her the dates of illnesses and surgeries. She knew of allergies, but could not possibly remember what meds she took for what, and if there were any weird reactions. Of course, she had another BOOK from her gynecologist, but she didn't offer that to the new practice, because she felt it was none of their business. The staff was attentive, they noted her concerns, performed an examination and sent her for blood work. Upon her subsequent visit, the doctor had little to offer. He had found nothing in her lab results or her physical. That "lump" she felt was gone, there was no presence of any disease at work. He did say that she seemed to be very anxious and he felt perhaps that was contributing to her feeling of illness.

Melinda still felt lousy but she had some relief knowing that nothing obvious was staring her in the face. She was offered different medications to try and mask the aches, pains and woes she was experiencing, but Melinda felt that they were a waste of time. She knew from past incidents that a drug for one part of the body inevitably screwed up something else. She was unsatisfied, and she would have to pursue specialist after specialist to take it further. She accepted the clean bill of health and was more determined than ever to "treat" mentally. To try and get her mind off her body, Melinda made arrangements with Charlene and Aviva to go out to a little Italian restaurant, and have a good time.

Sipping a glass of red wine, the three women started talking about the B&B business. Melinda was amazed at how well things had progressed from the start. Aviva was amazed that she had turned her life around so much and hadn't been this happy in years. Charlene was content that her mission had reached out to include these two good friends and made them an integral part of her life. As they sat and chatted, Melinda started to talk about the most bizarre people that had stayed at the B&B.

"There was one couple", Melinda began, "that brought their own sheets! When I questioned why, they said they didn't want to leave their DNA anywhere. Then there was a sleepwalker who went to the refrigerator all night long, at least 20 times and would open the door and just stand there. Oh yes, then there was a couple that had the loudest sex you have ever heard in your life! She was the screamer and he kept saying, good girl! Some pretty strange people."

Aviva added, "Oh yes, I remember one night when you called me on the phone Melinda because you were hearing funny noises and you wanted me to come down from my apartment. When I got there I heard them too! We were sneaking up the stairs hearing this jangling and saw the doors to the two rooms open. No talking, just some metallic sounds and swishing. We peeked into the first room and it was empty, at the second room we saw three men handcuffed, chained, and blindfolded and otherwise naked with three women dressed in leather, with God knows what their hands. It seems the men weren't allowed to make any noise or they would be punished. We wanted to laugh out loud but we didn't want to give away the fact we were there. It was too late , the women saw us. Instead of being angry, they were excited and asked us if we wanted to stay and play! I was so embarrassed I couldn't talk, you were as cool as could be. You thanked them for the invitation, but said we couldn't mix business with pleasure. You said goodnight and we walked back down! We were so confused because we had only checked in two couples, not three!"

"Oh that was a riot. In the morning, only two couples came down for breakfast as normal as could be . They said they had a great time!"

CHAPTER TWENTY-EIGHT

October arrived in autumnal glory. Preparations were underway for the wedding. There was only one more guest scheduled at the B&B and he was booked for 5 days in early October. Melinda felt that he would not be in the way of the preparation. The books were cleared then through November, because Dianna's baby would be arriving and she wanted unrestricted access to her daughter and grandchild.

On the morning of his arrival, Thomas Smith drove onto the property just as Melinda was gazing out the kitchen window. He was a man in his sixties. When he exited his car, Melinda could see a shock of gray hair and an easy stride as he collected his overnight bag and approached the door. She went to meet him, opened the front door and was faced with a handsome man that could have easily been a Hollywood star. For his part, Thomas missed Melinda's expression and slightly flushed face. She welcomed him and showed him to his room. She asked if he would like some coffee, or snack or even breakfast as it was only 9:30 am. He gladly accepted the coffee and a muffin. Melinda told him to come downstairs whenever he was ready, while she made the coffee and defrosted an apple cinnamon muffin from her stock.

About 10 minutes later, the aroma of the coffee and muffin filled the kitchen as Thomas walked in. He took a long swallow of coffee, bit into the muffin, and got the most satisfying smile on his face. Unity, who had been outside in the backyard, came back inside to check out the new person. She gave her whiff of approval and then sat down at her usual place, just to keep an eye on the situation.

"What brings you to Richmond, Thomas?" Melinda was trying to get the conversation going.

"Please", he said "call me Tom, and I am here to clean out my parents house. My mother insisted on staying in her house long after my father died. I had people looking after her for the last few years. In fact, it was the groundskeeper, Mr. Hendricks, who told me about your B&B. I've contacted an auction house to take care of the furnishings, some antiques, and there will be a yard sale for the smaller things. What doesn't sell will go to charity and the rest I guess it's just trash. I want to go today before any activity to get a couple of photo albums and personal things. The auction starts tomorrow, the yard sale the next day. Then the final cleanup. The house is officially on the market the day after."

"I'm sorry for your loss Tom. Did you live there as well?"

"Yes, it was my childhood home. It has both wonderful and terrible memories. After this business is concluded, I will never return here again. Melinda knew from that comment that something horrible had happened here. She decided not to pursue the conversation any further.

Before returning to his room and then leaving the B&B for the house, Tom asked her if she would like to see it. She was thrilled. Tom had mentioned that the house was close. In fact, it was so close that they could have walked there if not for the up and down hills of the area. At the first sight of the property, Tom was visibly shaken and Melinda was intrigued. The house had seen better days, but the structure was charming. It was much larger than Melinda was expecting. It sat in the middle of 5 acres on a treed lot. Although you couldn't see it, you could hear water running somewhere. It was apparent that the property had been well maintained.

Tom parked the car and they proceeded to enter. Because it had been locked up for several months now, since his Mother's funeral, it was musty. It looked like a period display from the 1960's. The first thing was to air it out, and let some light in. While Tom went to find his albums and documents, Melinda walked around the place, looking at the art, the books, the furniture and the general structure of the house. She just felt that at one time, this place was so loved. She could just feel the happiness that must have been here.

Tom returned with a bunch of things in his hands. Melinda inquired about some furnishings, about the neglected vegetable garden in the back of the house, and about the people who had lived here. Tom followed her and answered most of her questions, and showed her all the nooks and crannies that he used to play and hide in as a boy. His expression had gone from all business to memories of delight. This indeed was a happy home. In the backyard, Melinda found the source of the running water, it was a brook that ran across the left side of the house, originating somewhere along the property line, crossing over to a rock garden constructed to enhance the water sound, and then exited back at the property line, flowing into large drain pipes buried under the street at the front. It was so lovely.

"What happened here?" Melinda was trying to imagine why Tom would never wish to return here again.

"I haven't talked about it, because the memory is so hurtful," he said, " but I think I need to face it now, so I can say goodbye."

Tom went on to explain the events that led to his decision. " This was the place I grew up, the youngest of five brothers. My father was a Pharmacist and had an" apothecary" in town. He and my mother ran the whole place with transient " delivery boys". The store had a little soda fountain, and a tiny gift shop. This was way before the big chains came and took over the pharmacy business. People called him Doc and just like him, it

83

was a warm and inviting place. My brothers and I would sometimes go there and " help out", although I think we probably got in the way more than anything else.

We went to school, played sports, and went to church. We would fight over which TV programs to watch, or what game we wanted to play. Sure, we had our fights, but they were quickly resolved. Being the youngest was both a blessing and a curse. I got all the hand-me-downs, my decisions were the last to be considered, and I couldn't always hang out with my older brothers. Then again, I could demand more attention from my mother, I admit she spoiled me. As we got older, there was a question of who got the car, who had to go and pick up stuff Mom or Dad needed, who had to mow the lawn. I thought this was just typical family stuff, not realizing it was memories of good times being formed. Little snapshots of everyday things that you would later cherish.

We matured, and my brothers found wives and one-by-one moved away to start their own families. As each one left, whether for college or marriage, the silence grew in the house. It was still happy, but that great level of vibration that I loved just decreased. Finally, I was prepared as well to leave the nest. After college, I met my wife and we decided to leave Virginia for New York because we felt the opportunities would be there. I thought my parents would go into some kind of depression, or something! I couldn't have been more wrong. They were thrilled! Dad could see the writing on the wall, and knew his days operating his tiny store we're coming to an end. Despite the charm of his store, and the loyal customer base he had built up, he could not compete with Walgreens, CVS, and Walmart. It was the end of an era. He officially retired, and he and Mom started to go on vacations, and cruises, and even Photo Safaris! The only thing they didn't do was sell the house. After a while, I understood. Grandbabies! Holidays like Thanksgiving and Christmas took on a new life! Whenever possible we would be here to celebrate, and the clan continued to grow."

Tom's face suddenly changed, his expression went from someone delighting in wonderful memories, to someone anticipating dread and horror.

"My brothers and I decided to throw a 45th anniversary party for our parents. We chose a huge house in the Outer Banks to host it. 20 bedrooms and bathrooms, a banquet sized kitchen, a dining area, and a media room that could seat all of us! It was a block away from the beach, with a pool and a hot tub in the backyard. Preparations were worked out over a period of a year to get this together. At this point, my oldest brother, John, was 42 and his wife Janine had three children, my brother Luke was 39, and his wife, Laura, had two, my brother Matthew 36 and his wife Leigh, had 3, my brother Paul 32 and his wife, Cheryl had 2, and finally there was Elizabeth,

84

my wife and me. I was 25, we had no children, we were just trying to start our careers.

There were 19 people, traveling by chartered bus. My parents and I were taking my car because we had some stops to make along the way. It was a well-planned party with four days of ocean, sun and fun. The weather even cooperated and it looked like a fabulous time to be at the beach. Everyone met at this house. The bus arrived and we loaded in the suitcases, the supplies, the beach toys, the children's toys, and finally the people. We waved goodbye to the bus, and we got busy loading the car. Within 15 minutes, the house was closed up, the car was ready and we were off.

We started out and made a few stops along the way, gathering up some special goodies that we all loved. Then we maneuvered onto the highway which was bumper-to-bumper. The whole trip should have been about three, three and a half hours. Eventually the traffic just stopped altogether. I was hoping that the bus had gotten through this mess. Slowly, very slowly we started to move. About 2 hours into this hell, we saw the lights, and trucks ahead. Obviously, this immense slowdown was due to an accident, but until we were practically on top of it, we didn't realize that it was OUR bus. The details the cops on the scene told us, never sank into my brain. We just pulled over, screaming that it was our family on that bus and we wanted to see them. At that point, the ambulances had already taken many of them to area hospitals; those left onboard were already dead. Truthfully, I forgot about my parents and started screaming and searching for my wife Elizabeth. The police restrained me. The bus was such a wreck, it was dangerous for anyone to try and enter. I remember a jackknifed semi, I remember some passenger car torn to pieces, but most of all I remember that sick feeling, knowing my Elizabeth was gone.

"My parents were never the same. I was never the same. They mourned the deaths for the rest of their lives. Only staying in the house gave them peace of sorts. I stayed on for almost a year, but I knew I had to move on or I would be lost in a constant depression. When we buried our family right down the road, in the little graveyard at the church, I knew I would never have children because I couldn't bear the thought of another family going through such a horror. I thought of it as a protection to my sanity. I sometimes regret that decision, and other times think it was just the right thing to do."

Melinda did not feel that awful sentiment in this house, it just spoke to her of love.

"Tom, I know this is out of left field, but have you already signed a contract with a realtor?"

Tom was yanked out of his memories and startled by the question. " No, I have it all planned out, but not executed."

"If you don't mind," Melinda continued, " what is your asking price and could I show it to my daughter today?"

" Seriously?" he said. Melinda looked at him and responded, " I wouldn't have asked if I wasn't serious."

" Honestly," he answered, "I really have no idea, but yes, show it to her and see if there's even a deal to be made."

The two of them gathered up Tom's memories and drove back to the B&B in total silence.

Within an hour, Melinda had called Dianna and told her about the house. Dianna was eager to see it because nothing the agent had shown her so far appealed to her. Most houses were in cookie cutter neighborhoods where it was hard to differentiate one house from another. Noting her Mom's excitement , Dianna knew this house must really be something unusual. Looking at houses while hugely pregnant was quite a chore. Tom was not interested in going back to the house with the ladies, so he gave Melinda the keys and told them to enjoy the tour.

Dianna's first impression sparked her interest. The ladies went through the house very slowly, taking notes in every room, trying water faucets to check water pressure, and counting outlets in each room. Besides making considerations for decorating, painting, floors, rugs, etc, things looked good! They made a list of everything Dianna would want to change immediately, made notes about future projects, and wrote down things that could stay the same. They searched closet space, looked at appliances and mechanicals and finally decided the house was a gem. They calculated how much they would be willing to spend, and how much money it would take to fix all the things on the "immediate" list.

Dianna called Scott and he joined them at the house. Within 10 minutes, they were in agreement to buy the house. They looked around at the things in the house as well, and made a list of those items they would like to have. Melinda locked up the house, and the three of them went to talk to Tom.

It was a caravan of three cars heading back up the road. Best of all for Melinda, it was so close to her B&B.

CHAPTER TWENTY-NINE

As Michael's health improved, all his less attractive personality traits came back with a vengeance. He developed the attitude that if he couldn't own it, or have it, or take credit for it, then he would just fight for it. This included Melinda's B&B. If she wouldn't listen to him, and he couldn't manipulate the business, or the people she employed, then he was determined to insert himself into the situation until it became clear that she needed him so much that he would take the B&B off her hands to save the day. He was scheduled to go to Virginia for the wedding on the 10th of October, he planned to stay about a week, giving himself ample time to take charge. He had already planted the seeds with the local law enforcement that Hendricks and James were shady characters. Next he would try to impugn that Stan guy, the accountant. Michael was gleeful as he prepared for the trip. He would show them all.

  Michael always blamed Melinda more than his other wives, because as the first, and the mother of his children, she wounded him the most. He never understood what it was she wanted. She should have been happy for everything he provided for her. So what if he slept around, he rationalized that she wasn't that interested in sex or sexual games and she should be grateful that he didn't bother her. Truthfully, he thought his sex drive was just too much for any one woman, because of this he took pleasure where he found it. He was eager to assert his pressure to take back what he imagined as his.

CHAPTER THIRTY

Aviva returned to her apartment in the B&B. She knew there was one guest for the end of the week, and she was so excited to start and ready everything for the wedding. Stan had asked Aviva to marry him. She explained that she could never marry him because he wasn't Jewish! This made no sense to him, but perfect sense to her! Practically living with him, loving him and having intimate experiences with him, in her mind had nothing to do with marrying someone outside her faith. Stan, for his part, really wanted to call her his wife, but he knew he would have to settle for the partnership he had, and what he never thought he would actually attain.

Arriving at the B&B Aviva noticed the car and came in through the front door. Unity gave her a greeting, rolled over on her back for the expected belly rub and then went to her usual spot. Tom, thinking that Melinda had returned, came downstairs to find out what her daughter thought about the house. Aviva was startled, even though she knew someone was there. It was more Tom's appearance than his presence.

"Oh I'm sorry," he said.

Aviva recovered her composure and laughingly replied, "Oh , I knew someone was here, it's just that I recognized you from somewhere, and I still haven't placed exactly where that is. I'm Vivi, by the way and I help Melinda run this place. And you are.......?"

"Tom," he said, "he avoided her recognition remark, not eager to tell her where she may have seen him before.

"Were you needing something from Melinda? Can I help you with something?"

"No," he said, "I am just waiting for her to come back. I don't think she will be much longer."

" Great," answered Aviva, anxious to get up to her place. "If you do need anything before she gets back, just let me know." Aviva went upstairs to her place all the while wondering where she knew that gorgeous face from.

CHAPTER THIRTY-ONE

Melinda, Dianna and Scott returned to the B&B, eager (but not looking too eager), to discuss the purchase of the house. On the way, they called Ken Adams to ask about legal representation to buy a house in Virginia. Ken said it was no problem and he could handle it. When Melinda had bought the B&B, she had remembered simply going through a lawyer, but now she personally knew one!

As they pulled into the driveway, Melinda noticed Vivi's car. She wondered if she had met Tom, and if she had that same WOW reaction that she had. Tom was waiting in the sitting room. After introductions were made, everyone tried talking at once until they all started to laugh realizing that they were equally nervous and unfamiliar with the process. Tom decided to go first.

"I did a little research online while you went to the house. It is very difficult for me to part with it, even though I have wanted to have it done for years. If you are certain that you want to buy it, I have a price in mind. I think it is more than fair and I don't want to haggle about it."

Scott took over the conversation and told Tom exactly what they felt needed repair and that it would have to have a professional home inspection just to make sure it was sound. He indicated that they loved the house and would definitely buy it as soon as a price could be reached upon the results of the inspection.

Tom agreed with the terms and discussed the price which was agreeable to both parties. They drew up a non binding agreement and just like that the sale of the house was pending.

Dianna gave Tom a list of items she would like to stay in the house and he agreed to tentative prices for some of the larger pieces, such as the gorgeous dining room table and buffet. They all decided that they would return to the house, put yellow post it notes on the things that they wanted so that those things would not be sold at auction. Since it was getting late in the day, they all decided that after going back to the house again, they would seal the deal with dinner. They invited Vivi, she then invited Stan, and they settled on a cool, new restaurant in the city.

By the time the evening was over, it seemed like Tom had been incorporated into the clan.

On the way home, Scott blurted out, "I know who you are! You are Captain Cologne!"

"Captain who?" asked Melinda.

"You were the guy in all the ads , I remember seeing them on TV when I was a kid."

Melinda stared at Tom and had to admit, she had no idea who Captain Cologne was. " Does that make you famous?" asked Melinda.

"Well", said Tom, "Let's just say the Captain paid the bills and I guess for the most part still does! But please guys, don't call me that , I am just Tom."

Although they never called him Captain, or made references to the ads again, there were many, many little inferences that became a running dialogue and inside joke.

CHAPTER THIRTY-TWO

Five days before the wedding, all the plans were finally finished and the implementation of those plans began. Hendricks was busy planting cold weather pansies in all the borders along the driveway and walkways around the house. The lawn looked great and all the leaves starting to fall were constantly raked and disposed of. He was giving final finishes to bushes and getting ready to flush out the sprinkler system for the winter. In the back, extending the patio area, a large tent had been erected that could handle rain, or cold. It had portable heaters designed for the outdoors and looked like little fire pits. Tables were ready to be set out with chairs and linens but that would be last minute. The sides of the tent could be down, with openings that looked like windows if it was too cold. If the weather was warm, the side could be held back to look like parted curtains. Along the wall to the garage area of the house, where the patio ended, beautiful outdoor seating of a modular couch and chairs was placed with a large "coffee" table in the center. There was a makeshift bar as well. There were outdoor Tiki lamps placed around the furniture. There were about 60 people coming. The centerpieces for each of the tables were all set to be delivered the morning of the wedding, the china on which the dinner would be served was already stored in the kitchen, as well as the glassware. Mostly everything was a rental, and things were going smoothly.

James was giving the place a once over, making sure all the plumbing was working, that the generator that he had bought, and never used was ready to go if needed, and that the caterer had everything they needed. The catering place supplied waiters and a bartender. James had hired two teenage boys to park the cars, allowing for guests to have valet service right at the doorstep. He had made a plan, made sure that the boys completely understood and could implement it. When he finished with his obligations, he and Hendricks were each told to come for dinner at the party.

Michael was arriving today, and Daniel and Sarah, along with her parents, in two days. That would give everyone a little down time before the Saturday night party. Since the actual ceremony had already taken place, in Connecticut, and Daniel and Sarah were officially married, it made no difference who performed the ceremony. Charlene was so thrilled that the kids decided to ask her, as one of Melinda's first friends. Sarah decided to wear her wedding dress again, because she wanted Melinda, specifically, to see her in it. Then again, how many people get to wear a fabulous wedding dress twice!

Tom had stayed longer than anticipated and now the family was arriving for the wedding. He realized he would need somewhere to stay till the wedding guests left. He also realized Melinda was so preoccupied that she forgot that she had run out of rooms.

Michael arrived by taking a limo from the airport. He had brought two suitcases, one with the wedding clothes, and another with his everyday clothes. He never seemed to indicate how long he planned to stay. He seemed very agitated, far worse than his normal type A personality. He was talking fast, and went from one subject to another.

He walked into the B&B and immediately saw Tom.

"Who are you?" he demanded.

Tom extended his hand, but Michael did not reciprocate. At that point Melinda entered the room and caught a glimpse of what was going on.

"Michael, I see you made it! Have you met Tom?"

Michael's expression took on an angry look, " What are you doing here with my wife?"

Melinda and Tom looked at each other, "Michael, firstly I am not your wife, haven't been for many years, and secondly, you are in my house and I can have whomever I please to be here. Why don't you just go up to your room, and when you can gather yourself, come down and I will make introductions."

Michael seemed to refocus his attention, and realized at least for the moment that he was out of bounds.

"I thought I would be staying down in your room, I would rather do that."

He had only been there for 5 minutes and already Melinda was starting to feel sick.

"No Michael, we discussed this, you have an upstairs room, mine is not available"

Michael turned sharply towards Tom, and assumed he must be occupying Melinda's room, with Melinda. He internalized the misconception, grabbed his things and as he headed upstairs said to Tom, " this is not over."

Tom could see how shaken Melinda was and said, I know with all this going on that you forgot I had to vacate my room upstairs. Don't worry, I have another place to stay at the motel on Hull Street. She was really upset that she had forgotten, but she recovered and said, "You are right and I apologize. I also apologize for Michael and what you saw. Please promise me you will come back here after Michael leaves. Please too, if it's possible, join us for the wedding."

Melinda really wanted to say that she was interested in knowing more about Tom, and was hoping he was becoming a little more interested in her. She dismissed the idea almost immediately. She looked at him, and said to herself, "What would this gorgeous man want from me?"

He smiled at her, and promised her he would both attend the wedding and return to the B&B when the coast was clear, an intentional reference to the Captain.

CHAPTER THIRTY-THREE

Tom was the first to admit that he was really enjoying his time in Richmond. He was quite amazed that he felt so comfortable. He overstayed his initial five days, laughing at himself thinking that he could accomplish everything on a strict timeline. Nothing down here ran like clockwork. Besides, he was having fun being in the middle of the crazy B&B with all the characters down to the dog! Michael was the opposite of everyone he encountered. How could a person like Melinda ever be married to him ? How did she stay married to him? He was the most caustic person he had ever met. Melinda seemed to have a way of defusing his tirades, but Tom saw a streak of violence in him. Michael was even a contrast to Hendricks, with his gruff exterior and lack of verbal communication, but generally hardworking and harmless, and James who despite his background seemed honest!

While he was in the area, Tom called up some old friends. It felt good to reconnect although it was only for a brief moment. He did take a few hours to have a beer with his old friend Henry. He was shocked to learn that Henry had retired. Luckily for Tom, he was back in Richmond from Sarasota for a few weeks settling up some business. They got a kick over calling each other Captain. The conversation got around to Melinda and the B&B. Both men it seems were not only attracted to Melinda, but were fond of her as well. Although Henry had kept his distance, he often thought "what if?" Tom hardly knew her, he hadn't been around that long. He agreed though that there was just something special and terrific about her. Both men thought how ironic it was that neither of them would be staying in Richmond to let a relationship with Melinda blossom into anything significant. Henry had all but given up on the idea of a relationship with Melinda and Tom would be heading back to the big apple.

Later in the day, sitting in his room at a generic motel, Tom was deep in thought about Melinda herself. He gave her so much credit for recreating herself after being in such an abusive relationship. Not that she sailed through. He noticed how each contact with Michael would wear her down a bit, and that it was getting harder to recharge after each toxic comment. He felt that for some reason he was there, for the purpose of protecting her, although she would neither accept or expect that. He was careful to just keep it friendly with her, not give her any indication that he would like to get to know her better. His situation was too difficult to get involved with anyone, but if he could, she would be the woman he would pursue.

94

The wedding was tomorrow night and he realized he had nothing to wear! Such an odd thought, as he had tons of things to wear at home. It was just getting harder to picture his small apartment in Manhattan as home.

Home, why did it not strike a chord? He had done so very well for himself. When he and Elizabeth went to New York, they both were lucky to find work. Both of them were models. She primarily did print work, not too often on the runway. He was grabbed up quite quickly for the big Captain Cologne account that would keep him busy from the late 1960s to 1980s! He became the face of the company. With that exposure he went on not only to have his face spread across the TV screens, but on Billboard's, Subways, and magazines. But that kind of work is fleeting unless you can expand upon it. He had a long run, but in the end, the reign of Captain Cologne was over. It took a while for people to forget his name, but they couldn't forget that face! He was already doing modeling for clothing companies catering to men over 50. He was concentrating more on his walk and body. His hair turned silver and he was being portrayed in a new way. It was just enough of a change to freshen his image and he had a new audience to model for.

CHAPTER THIRTY-FOUR

Michael reluctantly settled into the guest room. He hung up his clothes and tried to calm himself down. He was out of control, and he knew it seemed to be getting worse. Normally, he realized he would delight in solving an irritating problem, but these days, everything was an irritating problem. He laid down in the bed. Although it was quite comfortable he felt compelled to find fault with it. Slowly he drifted off to sleep.

Thinking it had been but twenty minutes or so, he awoke with a start and noticed that the house was very quiet. He stood up, he was a little wobbly and chalked it up to the short plane flight. He also noticed that the feeling of anger was welling up once again. He descended the stairs and saw that it was already getting dark outside. The days were getting shorter and the clock was soon to be adjusted. As he roamed around the house, he became aware that he was quite alone. A note was placed for him on the kitchen table.

"We had some stuff to attend to. We didn't want to wake you. Will be back soon to discuss dinner. Hope you had a good nap."

The time gave him a chance to look around the place. He was wondering where they kept the booze. As he looked through cabinets and the pantry, he all of a sudden panicked that he had no car and couldn't get away from this place! He abandoned his search and went to the front door, flung it open and looked for a means of escape. He saw a vehicle approach, realized it was Melinda, and the panic started to subside. He saw, out of the corner of his eye, Unity was watching him. He hated that dog.

Melinda noticed Michael at the doorway. By the time she parked and entered the house, he was sitting comfortably in the living room.

Melinda took the opportunity to try and have a nice conversation with him. "Have you thought about dinner?", she asked. It's just the two of us tonight, I thought we could catch up."

Melinda saw for the first time that Michael looked tortured. His skin seemed stretched, and his coloring was off. His eyes kept moving as if a thousand thoughts were firing in his brain all at once. It seemed difficult for him to form a thought and hold it, instead he was prone to blurt things out. He knew that something was wrong too, but being the person always in control, he thought it must be everyone else that was causing him to feel this way.

" Why don't we start with who that guy Tom is?" he blurted out.

"OK" said Melinda, "that's an easy one. Tom came to the B&B to settle his parent's estate. His parents lived quite close and this was convenient. There was an auction for some of the furniture and art works. And then a yard sale, and finally he hired a company to clean out the rest. Ultimately the house would go on the market. Knowing that Dianna had not seen a house that suited her and Scott, I told her about Tom's parents house and we went to see it. It needs cleaning and some work, but basically cosmetic. She fell in love with it, called Scott and he came to see it, and the deal was sealed that night. Of course there was the price and inspection and stuff like that to settle, but all is working out nicely."

"OK", said Michael, "but what about you and him?"

"Nothing, Michael! He is staying here until things are settled, pays for the room he occupies and then I suppose he will go back to Manhattan. He is a very nice man, I enjoy him being here, he gets along with everyone, and that's it!

"What's wrong Melinda, not your type?" he said.

"No Michael, he is just my type, and if I was in the market for a boyfriend, or companion, or husband, I would pursue it 100%. But that's not what I want!"

Melinda wanted to add a lot to that statement, she wanted to say, she found Tom exceedingly attractive, she wanted to say that she felt marvelous when he was around her, and she wanted to say that if Tom ever gave her the slightest inclination that he was interested in her she would jump at the chance. All this she kept quiet, knowing in her mind, there were too many obstacles for that to happen.

CHAPTER THIRTY-FIVE

The day before the wedding, everyone had arrived and settled in. Sarah's parents occupied Vivi's apartment, Daniel and Sarah the second guest room upstairs, which had been Tom's room. Michael had reluctantly made peace with his upstairs guestroom.

Everything seemed to be in place, and all the vendors were ready. The only problem seemed to be that little things kept breaking down. Something was a little haywire with the yard irrigation system. It was actually time to shut it down for the season, but Hendricks just wanted to keep it open until after the wedding. He couldn't explain what had happened or why some of the flowers seemed uprooted. He complained, but kept fixing the problems. Inside, things seemed to be moved around, minor things in the kitchen broken, minor electrical problems, faucets that all of a sudden started to leak. James, like Hendricks, was annoyed and couldn't figure out what was going on. Nevertheless, he fixed it as it happened. James and Hendricks almost seemed giddy! They had never been invited to a wedding before! Michael was keeping as under control as he could. He was however, drinking more than Melinda had ever seen. She had never had very much liquor in her house, whether it was in NY or here. There was usually some wine, and a bottle of any hard liquor would last for years. Now, just because of the wedding, there was a lot of the hard stuff. She had let Scott, with some help from Tom, supply the liquor for the party.

The night before the wedding, the official rehearsal dinner, which was no rehearsal at all, Melinda, Michael, Dianna, Scott, Daniel, Sarah, and her parents, went out for an elegant dinner looking forward to the festivities tomorrow.

Michael asked his son to come and have a private talk. Daniel, thinking his Father was about to present him with a wedding gift, happily sat down next to him on the patio furniture outside.

"Daniel, it's a big step you are taking. You waited longer than I thought you would. Of course you realize that there will be a lot of changes to your life. I think at this point you should leave your job and come and work with me. As a husband, and I am sure, one day soon a Father, you need to make real money, not the peon stuff you currently bring in."

There it was, his big insult to Daniel. Michael continued, "unless of course, you want to live off your wife's earning. I think Dentists do fairly well! Anyway, if you want to be successful, you need the cash to match the image. Come and work with me. I can promise you will be successful."

Daniel was simultaneously irritated and happy! Michael always conflated success and money.

"What about your partner? Won't he mind the bosses kid climbing aboard"

"You leave Brian to me." Michael had a far away look in his eye.

"Dad, I am tempted but I don't think I want to end up with a heart condition and constant tumult just to rake in the money."

"Don't be a schmuck Daniel! I am offering you everything. Stop thinking like a small man. In fact, stop thinking about it at all. Go on your honeymoon, come home and just tell your place you quit! I expect you at the office the next day. How about we start you off with a salary. For a raw beginner I think 400,000 will do. I realize I will have to teach you everything. The stuff you do now is nothing compared to the work I do. Don't be afraid of it either, baby steps, just do what I say, don't pay attention to Brian, and in no time you will be up to running the place. You have to grow a spine. Sarah is a good first wife. You have to remember, even if there are subsequent wives, she will be the Mother of your children and that is sacred. You always take care of her and your children. The ones that follow are just eye candy. Be careful that there are no more children to support either. It's your time now Daniel.

Daniel was stunned. He left his Dad on the patio and went up to his room. He just couldn't process this information tonight. There would be enough time over the next few days. He did feel that finally he was going to make it big and people would look up to him, the way they did to Michael.

The day dawned, overcast and gray. There was a definite chill in the air. It almost dampened the spirits, but things got busy, and gradually the sun broke through and warmed everything up. At times it seemed like everything was dragging. The women fretted over their hair, the guys were trying to fit the wedding schedule in with the sports schedule. The key players, the florist, the caterers, the DJ, the parking attendants and the waiters, all got to the B&B and started transforming it. Charlene and Ken arrived and she went over the order of the ceremony. Hendricks and James looked so strange, but great, in suits. Hendricks was smiling, actually smiling. It was good to know he knew how! Unity looked splendid in her red bows! She quickly tired of greeting everyone and retired to her room to watch the proceeding from a window.

When Tom arrived, it took Melinda's breath away. She was almost embarrassed at the feeling it gave her.

At promptly 7 PM, the wedding began. Fashioned after a Jewish ceremony, there was a chuppa, or canopy under the stars. Chairs were arranged with an aisle in the center. Charlene walked down the aisle first, as she was officiating, and waited. She was followed by Dianna acting as the matron of honor, looking so radiant in her maternity gown, and accompanied by Scott, the Best Man. So many things were going through Melinda's head. She saw her pregnant daughter looking so beautiful, and she was so looking forward to the birth of the baby. She watched Daniel and Sarah starting off a new part of life together. She saw the love between Vivi and Stan, she saw Michael, in some kind of struggle she didn't understand. She was worried about him. She saw Tom, and she just hoped that he would leave her life very soon, or she would be entering a new phase, and she really didn't think she could handle that. Next it was her turn in the procession, she on one side of Daniel and Michael on the other. Her thoughts turned to her own wedding, when she had such high hopes of her and Michael joining and living happily ever after. She fervently hoped that neither of her children would ever know the depths of her unhappiness through those years. Finally, the bride and her parents. The three of them walked halfway down the aisle. They each gave Sarah a kiss on the cheek. Her mother and father proceeded to the chuppa, and Sara stood there waiting for Daniel to come and get her. Her gown was truly beautiful, and she looked marvelous in it. Daniel had picked a wonderful wife. Daniel met her in the aisle, and together they walked up to the chuppa. Charlene chose a few words about marriage, they exchanged vows that they each wrote, they exchanged rings. As Charlene pronounced them married, Daniel stepped on the wrapped glass and those who knew what to say yelled out Mazel Tov! It was a beautiful ceremony. Melinda's eyes caught Tom's expression. It was somewhere between sadness and remorse. Maybe it was too much for him to be at a wedding. She momentarily closed her eyes and said to herself, " I wish he would stay, more than I wish he would leave."

The area was quickly transformed into an outside dining area, there was a small area for anyone wishing to dance, and the feast began. Melinda was used to providing the food and desserts to everyone, but she had to admit that the caterer did an excellent job!

The wedding ended, the caterer cleaned up, the workers were paid and went home, the guests left, James and Hendricks said goodnight. Everyone went to their rooms and Melinda collapsed into bed. Unity came and snuggled against Melinda's legs. Melinda, who had made marvelous progress in controlling her physical symptoms through meditation, started to feel very sick. She had a premonition. When things go too well, there is something that comes along and screws it all up. Her mother used to say to her, "If you laugh before breakfast, you will cry before dinner," That line kept echoing in her head. She fell into a fitful sleep. Unity could not get comfortable with Melinda's twisting and turning and quietly moved away from her to a more comfortable position.

CHAPTER THIRTY-SIX

Ironically, the day after the wedding started out beautifully! A gorgeous autumn day in Central Virginia. Low humidity, a few wispy clouds in the sky, a lovely 70-degree temperature, and a show of leaves in glorious color. The woods behind the B&B were gorgeous, and the smell emanating from it was delightful. Birds, in quite a variety, we're busy searching for food or singing to one another. The Cardinals, the Blue Jays, Robins, Blue birds, Woodpeckers, Sparrows and Wrens. The Hummingbirds had gone South, and the feeders placed around the backyard had already been taken down. The wedding guests would be departing today. Daniel and Sarah would be off to their honeymoon. Not a big elaborate one, as each had to get back to work. They chose instead to go to DC and check out some of the many many museums and monuments, and stay at a hotel in the heart of the city. Sarah's parents would be on their way home. Michael was scheduled to leave first thing tomorrow morning. The children had also noticed the increase in Michael's erratic behavior and lack of impulse control. They had tried to discuss it with him, but he refused to even start the conversation. Vivi would be returning tonight and Melinda was glad she wouldn't have to be alone in the house with Michael. Before everyone got on their way, it was decided that they would go and check out the house that would be Dianna and Scott's new house. Michael refused, claiming he was too tired. Assuring him that they would only be gone for an hour or so, he seemed eager to be alone.

When everyone left, he was quite alone in the B&B, Michael went into the kitchen and grabbed the biggest knife he could find. The previous "pranks" he had pulled around the house in the last few days, did not seem to disturb anyone too much. He had been hoping to show Melinda and everyone else for that matter, that she could not run a business and that he would come in to rescue the day, but the vandalism he had caused was easily repaired. He had accomplished creating a nuisance and nothing more. Now he had a plan that would cast serious doubts on her abilities to run the B&B. Michael went outside to the patio of the house, the tent was still up, the extinguished fire pits standing alongside the furniture which was still arranged in the center of the patio. On each side of the sofa were heavy Tiki type lamps. Against the garage wall, near the placement of the furniture, was the electric box and the internet connection box. Michael thought that this would really do the job, if he could cut the wires from going into the house, all internet would be down and no one could then ask for

101

information, or book rooms. He thought it would take quite a while for anyone to find the damage because he would move the furniture over just a bit to cover up what he had done. He was giddy with the possibility. While everyone would panic, he would save the day and "find" the damage. Michael approached the wires, and frantically started swiping at them. It took awhile for the swipes to hit and he got wilder and wilder with the knife. Finally, he accomplished the task but in doing so, cut himself quite badly on the top of his left arm. He reeled from the shock of the cut, saw the blood pouring out, got a little dizzy and fell backwards hitting his head soundly against one of the lamps. The impact made him fall onto the patio, and in the process cut himself again across the thigh. As he lay there, bleeding, he realized he really had screwed up. He fell into unconsciousness.

Melinda and her departing guests came back to the B&B to pick up their belongings and go on their way. Everyone was excited about the new house, the new baby, the newlyweds and everyone trying to make arrangements to convene again at Thanksgiving. By that time, Dianna and Scott would be in their house, although it would still be a work in progress. There would be enough lodging for everyone between the house and the B&B. They arrived just in time to greet Vivi who had just stepped in. Melinda called upstairs for Michael. Unity came running in and started barking. She never barked, in fact other than her little growls of disapproval, she was the quietest dog Melinda had ever known! Now, she was barking and barking, she ran out through her doggie door. Everyone followed and saw Michael on the patio floor, blood flowing from his arm and thigh, knife still in his hand. The initial thought was that there must have been an intruder. Since he was there in the B&B there had been no reason to set the alarms. Melinda rushed to him. Daniel called 911. Tom called Henry and told him to get over to the B&B as soon as possible. He was hoping he would arrive before the officials got there. There was a pulse, and he was breathing, but erratically. Not knowing exactly what to do for him, towels were placed around the wounds trying to stem the blood flow. They had no idea how long he had been lying there. But there seemed to be a lot of blood.

Henry came racing in. He had gotten the call while he was in his car and only seconds away. He surveyed the situation and made sure no one touched the knife. He next went over to Melinda who was already being supported by Tom, and told her he had everything under control.

Although the paramedics and cops got there in a few minutes, Michael was gone. Even attempted CPR by Sarah failed to help him. The police took all the information they could, as no one was in the house when the accident happened. The knife was taken as evidence from the photographed scene. Almost as an afterthought, one of the cops looked at the wall next to the furniture and saw the severed wires. It was determined that it was the internet connection, and seemed to be purposefully cut.

"He did this on purpose," she finally said. "I bet he vandalized all those other things that kept happening this week. Why?" She was at a loss for an explanation. All the joy of the wedding festivities, all the preparation and money spent, all hopes for a happy future, dissolved in an instant. Michael had won. He had made everyone miserable so he could be the center of attention. This is what they would all remember.

As in all cases of unexplained death, an autopsy was performed. The results were shocking! It seems as if Michael's personality had been compounded by a brain tumor that had just started to express itself in his increased agitation. Who knows how long it had actually been there or at what point did it start to influence his more erratic behavior. This left Melinda in an even more conflicted state. Did she hate him so much that she didn't see the signs of a physical explanation? Did she want to confirm her hate for him, witnessing his outlandish behavior, and not questioning its source? Was she a horrible person because she wished him dead? Melinda slipped into a depression. For now the joy of running this B&B, this prospect of the baby, and the future of her own life was at stake. A new bottom. Michael had surely won.

Henry produced the file he had been keeping of the letters and accusations that Michael had sent about the B&B. He turned over everything to the new Captain and made sure that there was no suspicion cast on Melinda, Aviva, James or Hendricks. He spoke with Melinda for the next few days and assured her that she was in good hands with Tom there, but he would only be a phone call away if she needed him.

For the next two weeks Melinda would sit out on the patio in silence. She decided she just couldn't stand looking at that patio anymore. Within 2 weeks, Tom had it replaced with a new freeform stone one. It was really lovely. Hendricks landscaped the new area. Even so, Melinda would often retreat back there and talk, or yell at Michael. Charlene said the house should be "cleansed" to rid it of the bad energy that Michael had brought in. She conducted an impromptu, cleansing ceremony which was totally made up, but got everybody up swinging brooms and parading with candles. It was a good laugh, but did serve its purpose.

The atmosphere was definitely lightened. Although it was unnecessary, Dianna insisted that the B&B, get a new coat of paint in the downstairs rooms. A crew was hired and the job accomplished quickly. There was really no need, but who was going to argue with a very pregnant lady.

After Michael's death, both Dianna and Daniel were contacted by Michael's lawyer. It seems as if Michael had altered his will after suffering that heart attack. Things were in the process of being settled so that his will could be read and enacted upon in the upcoming weeks. Along with the actual will and the financial accounting, Michael had written personal notes and letters to his beneficiaries. The executor of the will would also have to approve any financial decisions made for the estate after the contents of the will was read, and the administration of the will would continue under his supervision. The contents of letters to Daniel Radnor and Dianna Radnor Lindley were documents meant for their eyes only and not to be shared with anyone including spouses. There would be a forfeit of money if the rules were not followed. One such letter had already been received by Dianna, the others would be distributed at the appropriate time.

CHAPTER THIRTY-SEVEN

Charlene came to the B&B at Melinda's request. She spoke calmly and offered these words. "No one can ever know completely the mind of another. The abuse you suffered from the many years you two were together, and his behavior over the last few months wouldn't have given you any indication. You said yourself, that he was drinking more, you know he was knocked for a loop after his heart attack. He realized he was just as vulnerable to illness and self-pity as the rest of us. He gave into his worst inclinations. Had he been a different type of person, he would have realized that something was wrong. He would have sought an answer and maybe the outcome would have been different. You were not part of the equation. The only thing you could do was keep your distance to preserve your sanity and not let him have sway over you again. He was toxic to you and there was no way of changing him. It happened, it's over and you must go on. He was the cause of the action. Don't be his reaction. We "cleansed" the property with love and light. He is no longer here.

Melinda took in what Charlene said. She was right. Melinda would not let Michael take up residence in her mind. He was truly gone.

Daniel was in a state of flux. Michael had made the offer, more like an ultimatum about his son joining his business. What now? Brian, the senior partner, knew nothing of this relationship. Would he honor it? Daniel had not given notice at his place of employment but also had not returned due to the death of Michael and all the drama that surrounded it. He was thinking of a way to talk to Sarah, but Michael had specifically told him not to involve her in business decisions. Daniel craved that status of rich, big man. How could he ever go back to the mundane job he used to love, but had reached the pinnacle with no hope of advancements. He was at a loss. Daniel decided to call Brian at his office.

"I wanted to discuss with you what my Father told me the night before my wedding. He offered me a job at his firm and even proposed a starting salary of 400, 000. I think I would like to take this offer. Of course, I realize that you are now the boss, but I am a quick learner and hopefully will one day be a full partner."

Brian either had no idea about this offer, or he pretended that this was news to him.

"Daniel, I have no knowledge of what you discussed with your Father, but there were no plans that I am aware of to bring you onboard the firm. Now that the situation has changed with his untimely death, I am not prepared to accept you in any position. I hope you can appreciate my predicament." With that Brian hung up. Daniel was irritated and doing a slow burn. "Dad, why did you do this to me? You made me an offer but your partner knows nothing about it and won't honor it! Shit!"

CHAPTER THIRTY-EIGHT

Tom woke up in the motel room he was temporarily staying at. The room was nice enough, the motel fairly new. Everything was in muted colors, the furniture nondescript. The bed was not the most comfortable, but serviceable. He smiled to himself when he realized how long he had actually been in Richmond. What he originally thought would take five days, had turned into weeks. How smug he was to think that everything would go like clockwork, according to the plan he put in place. He had nothing to rush back for. His condo was located in a posh part of Manhattan with 24-hour security. He could leave for months at a time, and had in the past, without any worry. He notified the security staff at his place that his plans had changed, and they could just continue to collect his mail. He told them to call him if there were any problems. Since Michael's death, Tom had stayed away from the B&B as Melinda had requested. He spent his time wandering around the city, looking at sites he actually had never seen when he lived there. He had contact with Dianna and Scott, checking up on their progress with the big move from their apartment to his childhood home, and offered his help. This, they gladly accepted. Events of the last week since the wedding had really taken a toll on Dianna. She took to bed as a precaution. Trying to coddle her, he became a surrogate father, helping in any way he could. He ran errands, went for food and helped clean everything entering the house, Tom had hired James to come and handle fixer up things, and there were so many! James refused money and said instead that it was a gift getting things ready for the baby. Each night he went back to the motel and collapsed into the bed. This is what it's like to be part of a family. Life in Manhattan started to feel very lonely and have no significance.

He thought about Melinda, he knew how badly she was hurting. She was probably torturing herself trying to find out why things happened the way they did, and assuming some of the blame. He understood perfectly. He had lived through the same nightmare. Sure, the circumstances were different but the pain, guilt and anguish were the same. He wished he could help her. If she would only reach out to him. And again, he knew he had started to develop feelings for her, but it was so premature to know if anything would come of it. He knew that she was unaware of his medical problems, he didn't like to admit that he had any. Last year he had been diagnosed with aggressive prostate cancer. He was devastated and saw his world falling apart. Although the doctors told him with surgery and treatment they could keep him going for years, he felt his life was over. He was the image of

"The Captain", and that meant, no physical weakness. Eight months ago, he had the surgery, with a couple of months of chemical treatment. While the cancer is temporarily halted, he lost the ability to achieve an erection, or have normal sexual relations. Doctors and therapists had suggestions of how to achieve sexual pleasure, but that required pills, shots, further surgery. He just couldn't go there now. There was also no one in his life at that point, so he thought he would just leave things as they were and concentrate on staying alive. The large 8 inch scar though, did bother him. Not that he did swimsuit modeling that often, but he still had that image to maintain. He rehabilitated his body, after the surgery, exercised his upper torso, and legs, and tried to keep that sculptured chest and stomach as best he could. Not bad for a guy his age, but he started to question why he felt he had to keep this ridiculous facade. He didn't need the money any longer, he was quite well off. Was it just an ego trip?

Now too, there was Melinda. He felt that she was a woman he could spend the rest of his life with. But what kind of life could he offer her? Would she be satisfied with his disabilities? When he was young and met Elizabeth the focus of life was to become famous and attain wealth. She was an absolutely beautiful girl. He was so taken by that body and face. They were married for almost two years when the accident happened. Most of those two years were spent working, traveling wherever the jobs were, and doing nothing but work. Even public appearances together was work. There was so little downtime, that they never really got to know each other. The question of children hardly ever came up and she couldn't afford the time to be pregnant. Real life was on hold, until professional life was conquered. The constant attention to diet, exercise, presentation superseded all else. On the rare occasion they could relax, they would allow themselves to eat something decadent, and sleep in late. That week at the beach was supposed to be that time. He realized now that he loved her image, and perhaps they would have learned to love each other, but in reality he didn't know her, and they never had the time. He questioned if he had the time now? He was so reluctant to talk to Melinda about this.

Just at that moment he got a text from Melinda asking him if he could stop over at the B&B. When Tom arrived at the B&B, Melinda was fortified with a speech and logically had listed talking points in her mind, But the minute she saw him all she could squeak out was," Can I have a hug?"

Without hesitation, Tom came over to her and held her tightly. Melinda started to cry. She had no control whatsoever. The tears just flowed as she held onto him. After a few minutes, she pulled away and with a half smile on her face said, "thank you." She led Tom over to the sofa, and as the two sat down Melinda said, " I had a whole speech ready, but none of it seems important now. Actually it flew right out of my head. I have no idea what I wanted to say." Jokingly he said," Well that's a relief, I thought you were going to tell me I owe more money for the room!"

Melinda smiled. "I just realized, the minute you walked in that I am so glad you are here. I had wished that there was some attraction between us, but now I realize that it was just a projection of what I wanted. In reality there is no us. You poor man. It reminds me of the show, Gilligan's Island, where you came for a few days, only to end up in a long drama. I'm so sorry you got caught up in all this, you had enough of your own drama."

"I'm not sorry," he said. "You and your family and friends gave me something I had lost a long time ago. Melinda looked puzzled. He continued, I came here with a task to complete. I have been carrying around a huge sadness for so many years. It affected everything in my life, and so many things I can never make up for, but when I came here and you prepared a muffin, a simple muffin, it was the first awakening to the memories that had been. We can never go backwards, but I realized that I had prevented myself from ever having memories, simple ones, like that again. Your warmth and enthusiasm, your excitement about your family and the potential of finding them a home. Your business at the B&B and the crazy assortment of people you have working here. Even down to Unity, who guards you constantly, and loves you immensely. When Michael came here for the wedding, and I saw how he treated you, I wanted to punch him hard. I knew I had to leave, because I couldn't stand witnessing his abuse to you. I realized I wasn't supposed to still be here but the truth was I didn't want to go. I hung around, not so much because of the house or the sale. I really could have done it remotely. I wanted to be around you. I was just biding my time till the craziness of the wedding was over and I didn't want to infringe upon you with your family time. You were correct before when you said, there is no us. We never had the time to make it about us. So my question for you is….. do you want me to stay? Do you want there to be an us?

Melinda almost fainted. "Tom as much as I would love there to be an us, how could there be? Excuse me please because I'm going to be very blunt. You, are a very well-known gorgeous personality, I, am well just me. What could you possibly expect from me when you are surrounded by beautiful people? I couldn't possibly compete, for the lack of a better word, with the dozens of women that would give anything just to be with you.   I already was in a relationship with Michael who cheated on me more than he was with me. Of course, he put the blame for that squarely on me, and he told me repeatedly, I couldn't fulfill his needs! I can't go through that again."

Tom was about to speak then stopped, and then started again. " Melinda. Nothing I say now will come out right. I have an analogy that I would like to tell you, but I want you to look at the meaning, not a direct comparison. Can

you do that? Melinda was confused but nodded yes. Tom continued, " I want you to think about birthday presents, or Christmas presents. There are usually some that are professionally gift-wrapped, others that are nicely done but plain, and some that look like a four-year-old wrapped them. When it gets down to the contents of the present, it really doesn't matter how it was wrapped. Some of those elegant packages have nothing of interest in them. Some are just gifts, without thought because somebody had to give you something. Some are great, others heartfelt. The package doesn't matter. I know you see me as a beautiful package, but this package before you has had a lot of help to look this way. Someday, I can show you the well hidden scars, about the hundreds of thousands of dollars needed to create and keep up this facade. Yes, I had the looks and the competitive drive when I was 20, but I wasn't given the opportunity to age naturally because of my profession. You were never given the opportunity to know how pretty you are. You bought into an idea that you have to look a certain way, not only by Michael but by society at large and people like me. As far as the contents of the present, what's under that wrapping, the two of us have an idea, but we really don't know because we haven't had the time to inspect it yet. We have expectations and hopes. Right now it's an attraction. Can't we give it a chance? I know you have ideas about me that I can't deliver upon, and I am sure the same is true for you. We are not kids anymore, I don't want to throw this opportunity away. Melinda, do you want me to stay?
Melinda was screaming inside her head, shut up you idiot and just kiss him! Instead she said, " I have many secrets, I'm not sure you will want to deal with them. I am a flawed person. But I try each day not to dwell on my inabilities. If you stay, and I so hope you do, you may find these things are too difficult for you to deal with. I will understand then if you ultimately have to leave. Tom, if you are willing to give it a try, I would be so happy."
At that point not giving Tom time to respond, she kissed him. The kiss was warm and passionate. After that it just stopped. Tom pulled away. "Oh no, thought Melinda, red flag number one."

CHAPTER THIRTY-NINE

The leaves were taking their time to fall this year. Everyday, the lawn was littered with the green, yellow, red, rust colors of leaves that had floated down from the trees that surrounded the property, but when you looked at the trees, they still seemed full of leaves that were stubbornly clinging. Some discussion had taken place about Thanksgiving, but Melinda was just not in the mood to entertain the whole crowd. It was unbelievable that two years had passed since the B&B came to life. Unity had rescued Melinda from a life without a loving pet and four years that saw the rebirth of Melinda from dreamer to entrepreneur. It was years of extreme ups and devastating lows. Some days had seemed interminably long, while the months seemed to just fly by. It was just at that moment that her phone rang to hear an extremely excited Scott, that Dianna's water had broken! Melinda called Vivi, Daniel, Charlene, and Tom. Tom was only about a half-hour away, on his return trip to Richmond, hauling his clothes and personal possessions. She told everyone where she would be and that the minute she knew anything, she would text the immediate world!

She drove so fast that when she ran into the hospital building, she had no memory of how she even got there. Quick as she could, she took the elevator to the maternity ward. There was no one there and no babies to be viewed. Desperately trying to find someone or something to give her information, she saw a corded phone on a desk with a number to call if you were waiting for a birth to happen. Before she could complete the call, Scott stepped into the room with the most wondrous expression on his face and said," Hi Grandma!"

Melinda tried to make sense blurting out five thoughts at once, but Scott cut her off, saying, "It's a girl! She's perfect, just like her Mama."

Melinda was so elated, and for one of the few times in her life, speechless. The birth had been a very quick one. Labor pains had started immediately after the sac had ruptured. Melinda and Scott had left the house within 5 minutes of the event. By the time they got to the hospital, when Scott had called Melinda, she was dilating and feeling strong urges to push.

It was so quick, unusual for a first birth that no sedative was given. The baby, weighing in at an even 7 LBs, and 18 inches long, came into the world calmly and easily. Scott had been in the delivery room and witnessed the whole procedure. The baby was taken by the nurses to be washed and put into a diaper and onesie, wrapped in a blanket, and placed in an isolette. Dianna was attended to by the doctor and nurses and then finally was allowed the formal introduction to her child. It was truly a beautiful moment that Scott meant to photograph but completely forgot as he was caught in the magnitude of the moment. Finally, Scott went to look for Grandma and introduce her to her Granddaughter in Dianna's room. Melinda realized that she had not called anyone! She pulled out her phone and started to text those whom she loved. Tom had just reached the B&B, turned out of the driveway and headed to the hospital. It was amazing how excited he was. He couldn't remember ever doing this for one of his nieces or nephews. He was hoping to be a part of this child's life. A name needed to be provided on the birth certificate. Dianna and Scott made a decision and refused to tell anyone. They said that when everyone who mattered was together, they would not only tell us the name but the reason behind it. All Melinda could think of was that they had given their child a name like Dimples or HoneyBun; oh, she hoped she was wrong!

CHAPTER FORTY

Once again, things weren't normal. Melinda had said from the beginning that she was not going to make a Thanksgiving dinner this year. That, however, didn't prevent everyone from being at the B&B. What was different, well, no Turkey and Stuffing, or Sweet potato pie, dinner was a variety of PIZZA! All kinds from vegetarian to the meat lovers dream! Some were sweet with pineapple, some very spicy and a lot of tame ones for those with less adventurous palates. The whole gang was there, Daniel, and Sarah, Tom, Dianna and Scott, and BABY, yet to be named, Vivi and Stan, Charlene and Ken.

Of course, Sarah's parents were invited, but they had made the decision to move from Connecticut to Florida and had just relocated there. After pizza was devoured and the baby had been passed around, it was time to hear the secret name. Dianna spoke, " We wanted our child to have the name of someone who had not had the opportunity to have the joy that we feel, and we also wanted to give this child an anchor to her family. Mom, we know what a difficult time you had with Dad, but you know that he really was a good father to us when we were growing up. His hostility was always aimed at you, and we feel terrible that we thought it was funny and did not intervene. It never diminished our love for you. Tom, you had a hole in your heart because of that terrible accident, and we wanted to repair it a little if we could. So, ladies and gentlemen, I present to you our daughter, Elizabeth Michelle. May she be a blessing to all of us. Tom sat stunned and then just started to weep. Melinda was really not sure how she felt about the whole thing. Everyone else seemed thrilled about the name choice. Melinda thought, "at least it is a nice name" Since Charlene was there, she performed a naming ceremony. She asked Scott and Dianna if they would name Tom and Vivi as the godparents. Vivi was honored but confused as Jewish female babies do not have godparents. Tom was so overwhelmed that he had to leave the room.

As dessert was passed out, basically make it yourself ice cream Sundaes, Melinda went looking for Tom. He had recovered at this point but was feeling so conflicted. Melinda understood immediately. "This has absolutely nothing to do with you and me as a couple. The kids apparently adore you and felt that they wanted to give you something special. In our tradition, godparents really don't do anything, so there is no obligation placed upon you. I had absolutely nothing to do with this. I was just as surprised as you."

"I was thinking about my Mother," he said, " imagine how overjoyed she would have been to see something like this. It really touched my heart. And yes, I know you had nothing to do with this, but I hate to tell you, every day, you are getting stuck with me a little more."

Teasingly she said, " I use pretty strong glue." She gave him a wink and went back to gobble down some of that ice cream.

Monday morning, a representative from Michael's firm, Bramel Assets Associates, came to Ken's office to read the Will. Michael had been a partner in the business with Sam Kleinman and Brian Schwartz. Sam had taken on Michael as a partner over 20 years ago, and Brian was a newcomer, with about five years on the job. Melinda had met Sam a long time ago on some social occasion but never met Brian at all. Sam retired about five years ago when Brian was hired. There were three secretaries; Michael used to call them the ABC girls because their names were Alva, Barbara, and Carol. Also on staff were two accountants and an associate who was a lawyer in the field of finance. There was never any contact between Melinda and the office other than phone calls when Michael needed to reach her or if she needed him. There was a dedicated phone line just for that purpose. Everyone had always treated her respectfully, and they exchanged pleasantries, but other than that, she knew nothing about these people. When Michael died, she received, along with the children, a letter of condolence and a contribution of 1,000 dollars to brain cancer research. Whether that contribution was ever made, she did not know.

Today was the first time she met Brian Schwartz. He once again expressed his condolences and then started on the provisions of the Will. After the first few years of their marriage, Michael seemed to be doing well. They lived comfortably but not extravagantly. As the business seemed to get more profitable, Michael seemed to get more abusive. It was especially apparent when his away time was far greater than his home time. Melinda sat there asking herself why she was present at this meeting anyway! She knew that Michael's other wives all had prenups, and therefore not entitled to any inheritance. Still, she really didn't think with her generous settlement that she would be given anything either.

Brian started reading a lot of legal jargon, which meant nothing to her, but then the number grabbed her attention. "The total estate is estimated to be 50 million dollars in cash, possessions, and assets. To my wife, Melinda, I bequeath 1 million dollars. The remainder of the estate is to be divided equally between my daughter, Dianna Radnor Lindley, and my son Daniel Radnor. The inheritance goes directly to them, and in case of divorce from their spouses, any money at that point stays with the principles. If my children precede their spouses in death, their balance goes directly to any children they may have. If the children, my grandchildren, are below the age

114

of majority, the account director from this firm will be appointed on how the money for the children can be spent. The children will gain control over their portion at age 21.

The choices of how to use the estate money will be monitored by the Bramel Assets Associates. Fees for accountants and lawyers have been prepaid, and therefore should not eat into the inheritance total. Taxes and other penalties that occur from time to time are fluid. Contingencies for these and other unforeseen costs have been taken into consideration. There are further instructions as to how to proceed, who to trust and what to watch out for." When Brian was finished, everyone sat silent and was stunned. Brian handed out printed material to Dianna and Daniel. Melinda was given an envelope. She opened it and found a handwritten note.

Dear Melinda, I amended my will after my heart attack. I thank you for rushing to NY to be with me, and the subsequent time I spent at the B&B. I know you will need this money because you can't possibly make it on what you earn at the B&B. This should give you enough to fix the place up, get a real business plan and have a little leftover. Don't be too upset when your playboy leaves you. Michael.

Melinda didn't know whether to laugh or cry. Odd, she thought, Michael sounded like he knew he was going to die, even though he obviously recovered from his heart attack. Why else would he cite the B&B? Melinda chuckled a little to herself, "now I have another nickname for Tom, The Playboy! Even in death, Michael, you are a dick!

Dianna and Daniel looked quickly through the papers they were given. They had glazed expressions on their faces. They were overwhelmed at the size of the estate and overwhelmed at the complexity of the will. It was going to take a lot of patience to work out what they should do next. One thing they both felt was that financial pressure was a thing of the past. That changed a lot!

Daniel was quietly seething. Why did Michael give Dianna equal footing with him? Daniel thought for sure that his pre-wedding talk with his father had promised him, and him alone the reins to the business and fortune.

Scott and Sarah sat there stunned. Michael had certainly written them out the Will. In addition, Dianna and Daniel seemed to exclude them from seeing any of the documentation or discuss any of the provisions with them. It felt odd and hurtful. Maybe everyone was just in shock.

Melinda went over to her in-law children. "Michael had no idea what family truly was. I know he had no other children with his subsequent wives, and he completely cut them out from anything financial. I can tell you from being married to him; they probably deserved something. Don't worry, you two. We are family, and you will never be cut out or left out. We will all be okay. I promise you.

Sarah gave her mother-in-law a big hug. Scott felt a bit deflated as to the importance of his own nuclear family.

The meeting ended. Everything contained in that Will was surprising, starting with the value of the estate. Sure, Michael did well, everyone knew that, but no one imagined how well. Of course, in typical Michael style, he gave her money because he disapproved of her "business acumen." Insulted her in a most passive-aggressive way, but at least the last laugh was hers because she didn't have to do anything at all to the B&B if she didn't want to. It was a moot point, after all. After the untimely death of Michael and the circumstances of his death, the B&B would no longer exist.

CHAPTER FORTY-ONE

As the family left the office and headed back to the car, there was no conversation. Each person was deep in thought and slightly stunned by what just happened. They had driven together after meeting at Diana's house.

Melinda was the first to speak. " I have a suggestion. I think each couple should make a list of the things they were planning to do as if nothing has changed. Then, look at that list and see what still is important and which things can be eliminated. Finally, make a list of things you were planning to do in the future, and see how important those things are now in light of the additional money. Tonight, I think the four of you should get together to discuss plans to see how much of it is a joint adventure, but also how independent you each want to be". Daniel looked puzzled. Melinda continued, " I want you to remember that money mixed with family can be very incendiary. There has to be some give-and-take, but things should stay as equal as possible. No amount of money is worth destroying a family. In the end, it is truly all you've got. Tomorrow night, hopefully after the four of you have some kind of plan or an understanding, let's meet at my house, and I will add my input."

Daniel asked, "Does Tom have anything to do with this?" Melinda responded, "not yet, he might eventually, but I am sure he's well off on his own. I really have to see how things progress."

Melinda grew quiet after this; she realized that as exciting as the prospect seemed that she would spend the rest of her days with Tom, there was something nagging at her. He had made speeches about her being pretty and desirable, but he never approached her romantically. Maybe, he really didn't find her so desirable at all. Then again, she had avoided appearing to be desirous of him either, basically because she was scared shitless about being intimate with him or anyone ever again. She decided when she got home, it was time for that discussion.

When Melinda got back to the B&B, she heard a racket going on in the kitchen. Tom was standing in front of the open refrigerator, pulling things out and placing them on the counter. He seemed so intent on his chore that he jumped when Melinda asked him what the hell he was doing! " I got a little hungry, and I was looking for something a little sweet, like a muffin or donut. I thought maybe it was in here, so I've been looking!"

Melinda giggled, " the muffins are in the other refrigerator in the freezer section. I haven't made a new batch in a few weeks."

"What other refrigerator? " he asked, puzzled.

"The one in the garage," she answered.

"There's another refrigerator?" He seemed to be very impressed. Melinda helped him put everything back and then escorted him into the garage; it seemed as if he had never been in there before. There was a regular refrigerator and a full stand-up freezer.

"When you run a place where you serve food, and you never know what you will need, you are prepared with at least a two-week backup! At least, that is the way I handle it."

" Come and sit with me. You can snack on this while I tell you what happened." She threw him an apple.

"You know-how behind your back," laughing a little, "we call you Captain. Well, now you're going to have to call me Heiress!"

Tom looked at her quizzically. "Michael left me a cool one million. Of course, the letter attached to the money was telling me what to do with it, but it was in the form of a nasty suggestion, not a directive."

"Wow, Madame heiress, that is great news and the kids?" He asked Melinda answered, "It was far beyond our expectations. I just hope they can handle it wisely. I have really no say in any of it."

As Tom bit into the apple, Melinda continued. It was so hard for her because she felt everything might come undone. She was really falling in love with him. It was ridiculous, they hadn't known each other very long, and somehow, he had insinuated himself into the core of the family. "Okay, here it goes," She said out loud. "Tom, do I repulse you physically, that is?" Tom's attention left the apple immediately! "There has never been an instance of physical attraction to me, not even an embrace, a suggestion of intimacy. Even the kiss we shared ended abruptly, and you pulled away. I know you have told me lovely things and tried to assure me that I am attractive to you. But Tom, why no action or attempted action? I have quite a past that you probably couldn't fathom, and I am neither apologetic for it or proud of it. But I do know that when a man has been at least a bit interested, he has suggested, if not acted upon, his desires for intimate contact. I am at a loss. Please, Tom, tell me what's going on? Are you gay?"

It hit Tom like a slap across the face. "Oh Melinda, you are so right. You deserve to know what is going on. Yes, there is a problem." Tom gulped, then continued, "Eight months ago, I had surgery for aggressive prostate cancer. The doc thinks we have it under control, and I am checked quite frequently for any recurrence. The problem is I can't get an erection. There are things I was given to try. But even with a short-lived artificial erection, I can't complete the deal. I have a huge scar that goes from my belly button to my groin. I can have scar revision surgery after a year, but I don't think I want to bother. I was trying to pretend that all was normal and that you would not notice or care. I should have told you up front."

Melinda was shocked by his confession. "I am so sorry. I had no idea. I assumed it was about me. In a way, it is about me. While you were trying to ignore this part of our relationship, I was doing the same thing. I am petrified about disclosing this, but if we are to have anything, we have to be honest with each other. After my divorce from Michael, I went wild. It was my poor way of trying to validate my life. I decided to sleep around with as many men as I perceived Michael had women. It was debasing. I started hanging out with all kinds of characters, into all kinds of things, thinking I was controlling everything around me. There are a couple of guys who decided I could be an asset to them. They tried to woo me into being a paid escort for them. It was unusual, they said, that in my age group, I was in my early 40's I could both tempt a guy sexually and hold a conversation. I laughed and told them I did what I did for myself and certainly not for money. Also, I said I would never do that to enrich them. To condense a long horrid story, I was abducted, drugged, and repeatedly raped. It's almost a blessing that I can't remember most of it. I was dumped at a hospital ER, where thankfully, I was treated. The doctor said it was the most brutal rape he had ever seen. There was so much damage done that I needed an emergency hysterectomy. There was a lot of blood loss and permanent damage. Although I certainly followed through with police reports and detectives and anything else I could think of, no one was ever arrested. No one was even accused, and it went cold. The men I had known were connected with both politics, and I believe, the Mob. Since I was divorced, I could keep this all from Michael because he would have made the rest of my life hell. I told my kids about the hysterectomy when I was almost fully recovered, saying that it was due to a ruptured ovarian cyst and that there were complications of fibroids. No one ever questioned me. Of course, I blame myself for putting myself in that situation, and my stupidity, but not, of course, for the attack. You are the only person, other than the doctor and the people working on the case, who know about it. As a result, intercourse is painful and now, years later, all but impossible due to atrophy of the tissue. I was willing to bear through it if it would have made someone happy who I cared about. I know that's stupid, but I thought I would have to try."

Tom was horrified. "Never, Melinda, for me or anyone, go through that kind of pain. Melinda looked at Tom but couldn't read his face. Finally, she said, "So is there ever going to be any intimacy? Can we learn how to be with each other without feeling bad about it or physically hurting?"

Tom got up, took the half apple and threw it in the garbage. "There is no time like the present." He gently took her arm and led her into the bedroom. Unity sensed something and quickly got off the bed. Each of them began to undress, both so uncomfortably. Tom's eyes were on her constantly. Had she known how today would go, she might have worn sexy underwear. Melinda, for her part, watched as Tom peeled off his shirt and pants. Even though she was prepared, she gasped a little at the long incision. It still looked raw, but he told her there was no pain. Despite the scar, the man was so beautiful.

Tom approached her on the side of the bed. He stepped close to embrace her, but in doing so, he stepped on her toes. She looked down then quickly raised her head. Tom, feeling her toes under his foot, also looked down, and as a result, Melinda's head snapped up and hit his jaw, which then caused him to bite his lip hard! He tasted blood and, still standing on her toes, turned his body to the night table where he saw a box of tissues. Melinda trying to extricate her foot, didn't see his right hand swing up as he turned. It landed a blow to her nose, which also started to bleed. When the two of them realized what happened, he with a bloody lip and she with her nose flowing, they burst into peals of laughter and fell on the bed. Before either one of them could control it because of their physical conditions, the laughter caused them to pee all over the bedspread.

The absolute ridiculousness of the situation caused them to laugh even more. When they finally calmed down, Tom rolled over on his side and started to kiss her gently. At first, the thought in Melinda's head was, "OMG, the bedspread!" But within seconds, nothing besides Tom mattered. She returned his kisses, and they grew in passion and intensity. No one needed instruction. Instinctively they knew what to do and where to do it. It became easy just to say, "No, not there, or that feels great!" There was no more embarrassment. She knew at that moment that despite the short time they had known each other, she was in love.

CHAPTER FORTY-TWO

Monday and Tuesday were busy with plans, ideas, hopes, desires and a dose of reality. Each couple spoke alone, then with the others. Finally, prepared with lists and talking points, they all came together at the B&B to reach some conclusions. They were all aware that even when things look great on paper, they rarely work out that way.

Tom and Melinda also had serious conversations about how to handle their finances, as Melinda insisted Tom's money be kept separate from the Radnor family pool. Tom understood and wanted to make sure that he was not expecting nor needed Melinda's money, but he felt that as a part of the family, even though not officially, his suggestions should be taken seriously. He was not asking to be part of the greater bulk of the estate, but he most definitely wanted a say in whatever concerned him.

Melinda started off by asking everyone if they had a basic plan of attack and were they all on the same page. The kids assured her they were. "Good," she responded. "I will start and see what you think with my plans. You asked me yesterday if Tom was part of this plan. We can only say yes with the caveat that we will not get married so that nothing in our finances ever gets jumbled. We have decided that the outside world doesn't need to know our business. They can think whatever they like. I had indicated that because of the way your father died, I can no longer run this place as a B&B. I just could never be comfortable, but I do want to stay here and make a couple of alterations to it." Tom spoke up at this point, "I plan to move in here. I hope there are no objections from you. If there are now would be a good time to voice them." Tom and Melinda looked at each person in the room while they waited for objections. "Okay," Tom continued, I intend to help your mom renovate the upstairs. I am going to convert the two guest rooms and bathrooms into one suite. I am keeping my apartment in NY. We can all use it for trips into the city, business, or whatever it needs to be. It also is a place I can return to if this doesn't work out, although I don't see that happening."

Melinda took over the conversation again, "I have to talk to Vivi. You know what she means to me, and if she absolutely needs to keep her apartment here, there is no problem, but if she is ready to join Stan full time, it would be a perfect time to do so. I will assure her that it is there for her whenever she needs it, and if something ever happens to me, I would hope you would honor that. Now, since I will be losing the little income from the B&B, I, and I mean WE," as she looked at Tom," have come up with an idea that I think we will enjoy. I am going to continue baking muffins, cupcakes, donuts, cookies, and sell them by request only during the fall, winter and spring months. I have a little following here, and we can mail out some flyers and call those who have bought from me before. I already have a license to operate, and I will be able to do as much or as little as I want to. We have a name and a face for the business, using the person who seems to like my baking the most. So I introduce, "Captain's Cookies & Melinda's Muffins!" Artwork and packaging to yet be created.

Everyone got a good chuckle as Tom stood up and gave a flourishing bow as the conversation turned to the kids. Daniel seemed a little hesitant, but he spoke next.

"Mom, Tom, there is one thing that might just interfere with those plans. Since the inheritance significantly changed our plans, we were hoping to leave Connecticut and the rat race there to come here! Sarah's parents have moved to Florida, so there is no reason for us to stay there now. We were hoping to build a family house here on this property as a multigenerational house. We were thinking, and I don't mean to sound that you are old and not able to handle things yourself, but eventually, that might be the case, and we would all like to be here for you." It kind of took Melinda by surprise. Were they already viewing her as too old to handle her own affairs? Did they think she needed a chaperone? Were they so sure that Tom was going to fly the coop and she would end up alone?

"Daniel, I think that is a wonderful idea, but I think you don't have to sacrifice the B&B to achieve it. The property is large enough and wide enough to construct a rather large house perpendicular to this one. In fact, it might look very charming if you keep the architecture the same. It will seem like a family compound. That way, in the event of a future need to be close to Mom, you will have her already established in her own place, with plenty of room for caretakers. It sounds terrible, Melinda, I know, but eventually, if we are lucky to live that long, it might be necessary and a Godsend to know that you will be able to remain here. Because the garage is on the edge of the house, it would be very easy to adjoin the two structures so that they can remain independent. Yet, you can go from one unit to another without having to access it from the outside. It makes it safer too. We can incorporate some of that into our renovation by installing an elevator in one of the garage bays to access the second floor. That way, you," pointing at Melinda, "or I, don't have to navigate the stairs when that might become difficult."

Melinda saw that Tom was trying to diffuse the emotional reaction that was brewing in her. It worked, and she was able to respond with a smile and muster up some excitement by telling Daniel it was a wonderful idea. Although this had not been the thought that Daniel and Sarah had, they were wise enough to consider that Melinda, and Tom, for that matter, were not ready to give up their total independence. Furthermore, plans for such a project could take about two years!

Dianna spoke next, but briefly, she deferred to Scott, which Melinda thought was wise. No way would she want Scott to feel that he wasn't an integral part of the decision-making. Scott was just coming out of his annoyance at Michael for keeping him out of the inheritance.

During this whole family conversation, Elizabeth was sleeping soundly in a baby carrier. When the conversation ended, it seemed to be a cue for her to wake up and fuss. Tom was the first to reach her and gently lift her out of the carrier. He took his role as Godfather very seriously!

CHAPTER FORTY-THREE

What Melinda thought was a constructive discussion was far from settled in Daniel's mind. He grew increasingly irritated at Tom and his solutions to what Daniel perceived as problems. He was moody towards Melinda because he felt she was undercutting his authority. It was also irritating to him that Scott didn't loudly profess his agreement with Daniel's plan. It was festering in Daniel as Tom interviewed architects, and builders, presented drawings of what the house could look like, whether there were any legalities about having two dwellings on a single plot, etc. Ken was handling the legal work, and Stan crunched the numbers. As far as the B&B, Melinda and Tom got busy right away renovating the second floor.

There was more than just the housing that bothered Daniel. Daniel had never told anyone about his talk with his father the night before the wedding. With Michael's death, he knew that Brian would not welcome him to the business with open arms. When the will was read, Daniel thought he had hit the lottery and was now in control of a fortune, only to realize he controlled nothing. He, too, was peeved that Diana had been given equal access to the money. Daniel convinced her that he would handle everything and just keep her apprised of the decisions he was making. Diana, for her part, was okay with this as she didn't want Scott to feel that he was unimportant while she and her brother were making all the financial decisions.

Tom had a post office box where he received his mail. Daniel was curious as to why Tom didn't change his address for mail delivery to the B&B. Was he hiding something? Daniel became obsessed with Tom and his relationship with his mother. He made inquiries through his new position as co-chairman of the family estate about Tom's finances and other business dealings. What he found was not at all what he was expecting.

Winter took a long time to come, but when it did, it came with a vengeance. Dianna, Scott, and Elizabeth, now joined by Poochie, the dog, and Jumbles, the cat, were nicely hunkered down in their house. They had hardly touched the surface in their renovations but were warm and comfy. Dianna was concerned about the subservient position that Scott had been placed in, and Daniel became a little more distant from him every day. She saw the signs that Daniel was turning into his father. She didn't know how to handle it. Scott, for his part, felt like he was losing his sense of self-worth. He was thinking about going back to his original position, working from his home office and leaving the Radnor Estate to Dianna. He was waiting for a good time to discuss this with her. In the meantime, in his own home, with his wife, daughter and fur babies, he was happy and content. Honestly, he couldn't understand why Daniel was so irritated by everything that Tom suggested or did.

Daniel and Sarah were renting an apartment. Daniel especially hoped he would only need a year's lease. Sarah had taken Melinda's suggestion to heart and had found a position in a local dental office. She was a welcome addition to an all-female run practice that was becoming very popular. They understood her desire to be part-time, and she agreed to work twice a week, in an 8-hour block. Daniel, for his part, took this position with a grain of salt; if it made her happy and he didn't have to hear her complain, it was fine.

Daniel felt content to be the manager of the 50 million. At least, that is the way he wanted to perceive it. He could not make any individual decisions and had to run everything through the estate manager. In one way, he felt he was fulfilling his role as the successful entrepreneur, but he hated the idea of being subservient to anyone.

Finally, the Holiday Season was fully upon them. Elizabeth's first Christmas, and Chanukah, and Kwanza too! The B&B was decorated. Melinda had prepared a beautiful buffet dinner, and everyone came loaded with wrapped presents. Melinda had a fleeting thought in her mind about Tom's speech about the wrappings on presents. It was truly in her mind that the gifts were heartfelt and not just pretty packages.

The guests arrived all dressed in PAJAMAS! It was decided that everyone wanted to be comfortable. Since this was a total jumble of people, each with their own attachments to the different holidays, they were going to enjoy it their way! Of course, these were not your every night pajamas; they were carefully chosen to reflect the people who wore them. Holiday pajamas had become quite popular in the last few years. Dianna and Scott, and Elizabeth wore a snowflake design. Neither Poochie nor Jumbles attended. Daniel and Sarah wore Rudolph pajamas complete with red noses! Ken and Charlene came as packages. Vivi and Stan as Menorahs, and Tom and Melinda as Mr. and Mrs. Claus, complete with big bellies! The funniest pajamas of all were when James came in pajamas made to look like a tuxedo! He skipped over the holidays and went right to New Years! He was encouraged to stay for the evening but bowed out. He owed everything to these people but was not comfortable to stay. The gesture that he came at all made everybody happy, especially the 15 minutes he got to spend with Unity. Hendricks absolutely refused the invitation but sent over a huge poinsettia! Last but not least, Unity herself was in an angel doggie costume, which she wore proudly for 15 minutes and then, in true Unity style, retreated to the bedroom and tore off her costume.

CHAPTER FORTY-FOUR

While a temporary truce existed during the holidays, when things returned to everyday life, tempers started to flare again. Tom presented to everyone the drawings that two architects proposed. In addition, there were sets of floor plans. Before everyone could examine the documents, Daniel erupted and said. I don't know why you proceeded with this. It isn't at all what I want. It was as if someone had just zapped them all with volts of electricity. Melinda quickly said, "What do you mean, what you want?"

Daniel was flushed and angry. I thought you understood from the beginning that I want to build a multigenerational house where Sarah and I and our future kids would have the house of our dreams. We would give you an area, an in-law apartment. I think they call it that." Tom started to rise, but Melinda stopped him. " Oh, I see," she started slowly, " you want to destroy my home, that I love, on my property, to give you exactly what you want. You will throw me a bone by giving me, and I suppose Tom too, a suite to keep us in a corner of the place. You will make sure we are well contained. You never considered what I do, with the kind of space and kitchen I need. You never considered that I love to sit on my porch or my patio to enjoy the woods. You haven't considered at all that Tom and I have our own quarters, and that's the way we like it. " Melinda's voice grew louder with each word. "Are you going to try and declare us incompetent along the way so you can then control where we walk and what we eat!" Daniel looked as if someone stuck a pin in him, and he deflated. "I was only trying to do what is best for everyone." He quietly replied. "Great," said Melinda, "but not by asking anyone else what was good for them!" Daniel seemed to remember something which gave him a second spurt of energy. "Oh, you think you know everything about Tom, you think he is such an upfront and honest guy. Well, I've had some investigating going on. I was curious why he has a post box and does not use the B&B as his address. He receives all kinds of packages and mail there. I think there is something to really look into there; it is very curious. I am trying to protect you, Mom." At that point, both Melinda and Tom burst into laughter.

'You are right, Daniel. There is something nefarious going on." Melinda was giggling under her breath. You see, I have been conducting a secret business from the post office because I didn't want people to know where I live. Have you ever heard of the name Keith Elder?" Tom looked around the room and saw recognition in Sarah and Dianna. "

"You mean Keith Elder, the guy who writes the short stories?" Asked Dianna.

"Yes, that's the one. Well, Daniel, sorry I have been hiding this awful secret from you, although your mom knew Keith and I are one and the same. I have been writing short stories since I was in college. I knew that the chances of making it big in modeling and advertising was an unlikely thing, no matter how good you think you are. I was an English major in college and have always written short stories. I submitted the first group of stories right before I landed the Captain Cologne account. I had great success with it, and I continued to write because I love it, and you never know when things like the Captain are over. My schedule gave me tons of time to write. Over the years, I have had ten anthologies published. That is my big secret! I can see why you have been so upset about this!"
Once again, Daniel was deflated.

Out of nowhere, Scott arose and said to everyone, although it was aimed at Daniel. " You were warned about the things money does to a family. While I believe initially you had good intentions, you started to become totally self-absorbed. Everything was what you wanted; everything was to be done your way. While I realize Dianna was trying to make me feel that I was an important part of this family business, you gave me no responsibility and never asked me for my opinion. I was to be your yes man, even if I disagreed totally. Well, it's not going to happen. I am going back to my little job, where I was valued. Since I have no stake anyway in the family business and your father obviously didn't trust Sarah or me with any of the money or decisions, I quit!"

Before Daniel could respond to this outburst, Dianna and Sarah gave him a cheer!

Everyone just got up and left Daniel stew for a few minutes. Sarah walked back into the room and sat beside him. "Daniel, you know I love you, and you know that this dream inheritance has changed you. It's not too late. Please don't go down this road and tear us all apart. I am not picking on you. Just think calmly for a minute, did you ever ask me about what kind of house I wanted? Did you ever consider the needs of your Mom and Tom? Why are you so intent on discrediting Tom? Why do you feel the need to tear other people down? I was so proud of Scott right now. Please don't reduce us to lackeys working for you. I suggest you get some help, learn why you are acting like your father. We loved you just the way you were. We were proud of you to take on the project of handling this wealth. We never expected or wanted you to become a tyrant because of it."

Melinda was listening in to this, although they didn't see her. She waited until Sarah left and approached her son.

"Mom, please don't unload on me too."

128

"Daniel, my boy, I am not going to do that right now. I am just going to say that I love you. I know who you are, and I believe in you." Without saying another word, Melinda gave Daniel a kiss on the cheek and then walked out of the room.

Daniel sat still for a few minutes; all of a sudden, it hit him! Oh my god, OH MY GOD! we've been scammed. It dawned on him that the "Letters" he was presented after the reading of the Will and the guidance letters he received ever since could not have been created or generated by his father. The person controlling the money at the top couldn't really be directing the estate. Something was wrong. He found Tom and asked him to walk outside to help him clear his head. Tom agreed although he couldn't imagine why. As soon as they cleared the front door, Daniel told him he thought the B&B was bugged. At first, Tom thought Daniel was having a mental breakdown, but as Daniel continued to tell Tom about the "letters" directing him to do exactly what he was told or lose money, Tom also became suspicious. Daniel said that not only did he get instructions, but Dianna did as well. One of the stipulations in the Will was that they couldn't discuss whatever the letters said. Some things started to click in Tom's head. Daniel apologized for everything that happened since the Will was read. But he really thought he was protecting his family. Tom couldn't think of a reason why someone would be putting the family through this. What do they accomplish from this? He had an idea how to proceed. He needed to speak with Dianna.

      The guys came back inside, and Tom announced, totally out of character, that he wanted an ice cream sundae from Cold Stone, and he insisted that everybody come. He made Dianna get the baby bundled up, pried Melinda out of the kitchen. Told Sarah that sweets were bad for the teeth but good for the soul. Eventually, he had everyone out of the door and packed into three cars. At the ice cream store, he gathered everyone around. "We think we have a big problem," pointing to Daniel. "I understand Daniel's reluctance to speak up about this because he thought he was protecting the family, but what he told me is very disturbing. Dianna, were you sent letters by the so-called estate executive?" Dianna turned red and admitted she had. "Were you also told in those letters not to discuss anything, even with your husband, or you would be penalized and have your inheritance reduced." She slowly nodded yes. "Okay, I think the B&B is bugged. Someone is keeping tabs on everything we say. I think when you", pointing to Dianna, "insisted on having the B&B painted, they put them in. That's the only time it would have been possible. There is something fishy going on here. I think I know what we have to do. The only thing I am worried about, for all of you, is that the money you thought you had and were protecting may not be there at all. Dianna, please tell us what the first note said."

Dianna looked sheepishly at Scott. "At the reading of the Will, he told me not to discuss anything with Scott. The less he knew, the safer the money would be."

"The next note?" asked Tom. " Oh please, do I have to? I feel like a jerk."

" It's okay," said Tom, "we're solving a problem here. No one is going to be angry at you."

"Okay," She continued, " The next note was to name the baby Michelle or Michael. When we named the baby Elizabeth Michelle, I got a nasty note saying that the next time I defied my father's wishes, I would lose some money from my inheritance. That dad was very clear about his wishes. Finally, the last note told me to have the B&B painted. Oh my god, I knew it was weird, but I thought it was real!"

"Everyone, can you see, whoever this is, they are trying to put a wedge between all of you. The deductions in the money go where? Who is punishing you in the name of your father?"

While the group went into Cold Stone, Tom made a couple of phone calls. He was a firm believer in starting with people you know. The first call went to Stan. He told him they needed a forensic accountant and why. He asked him if he knew of anyone. Offhand, he didn't, but he certainly knew where to look; he would get on it and handle it. The next call went to Ken. After telling him what had been going on, Ken admitted that the whole handling of the will was odd. Since he was simply letting the so-called "lawyer" from the estate use his office, he felt it was not his business to speak up. However, he knew exactly what to do and who to contact at this point. The police would not be equipped to handle this type of white-collar crime, but Tom thought it would be best to let them know that the house was bugged and that, indeed, a crime is being committed. Tom called Melinda Clark and told her of the problem.

It was agreed that they should leave the bugs in place and just not talk about anything significant. It was decided that no one should gather at the B&B about business and stay clear of any discussion of plans or money till the investigation was over. All plans, except for Tom's renovations of the second floor, were temporarily on hold.

It seemed amazing to the family that they could have been duped so easily—never questioning orders being given through notes or letters with punitive results for disobeying. It seemed so ridiculous. Had someone else fallen prey to this scam, they would have ridiculed the people for being naive dopes! However, it was them, and they would have to live with it and hopefully learn from the experience.

The investigation grew ever wider and wider. Eventually, the FBI became involved. The Radner estate was a small scam among the many really large ones. It seems that Sam Kleinman had committed some major crimes, and Michael had discovered it. He blackmailed Sam to hide the crimes and caused him to retire. The new guy, Brian, was a friend of Michaels, he was part of Michael's scheme, and he expanded upon it. While Michael would manipulate numbers to his advantage, Brian included threats and manipulation to increase his take. He would understate the value of the estates and take a percentage off the top.

Unless the finances were gone through with a fine-tooth comb, no one missed the million or two. In addition, If the clients wished to use any of their own money, all projects would have to go through him, where he would provide his own people to accomplish what they wanted, whether it was a purchase such as a plane or the installation of tennis courts and pools. That way, the cost of the project was in his hands, and the final price would contain a hefty bonus for him. It was easy for the experts to nail him on extortion, embezzlement, and racketeering. The money taken out of people's estates was shifted to offshore accounts. Shell companies were created to look as if business was being done with people's money. No one except Michael and Brian ever saw a profit. They were careful not to take too much from any one account at any time, to make it appear that it was just a downturn on people's principles. It was a slow drip technique, never siphoning off too much at any one time. The theatrics with the notes and letters were just a tactic to gain control over their emotions, promote distrust of family members, and provide enough chaos that would help Brian control the situation. Now that Michael was gone, Brian felt no allegiance to Michael's family and wanted as much as he could get.

The forensic accountant and the FBI tried to get an accurate reading of just how much money was stolen from the many accounts. In the end, what they could recover was a fraction of the original amount. Brian went to jail, his license revoked, but with white-collar crimes, he legally couldn't be punished enough. Melinda was able to keep her million because it actually came from an untouched account Michael had never manipulated and kept private from Brian.   The kids, though, saw their amount quite diminished. Still, they received a nice sum of three million each, which wouldn't totally alter their lives but just made it more comfortable.

CHAPTER FORTY-FIVE

The Spring gave way to Summer, and after a brutal winter, Spring and summer announced themselves with the worst amounts of pollen. Everything was covered by green dust that clung to every surface. Renovations to the second floor of the B&B were completed. The new layout gave Tom the space he needed for two walk-in closets for his clothes and shoes and one large closet for his manuscripts and writing paraphernalia. The bathroom was updated from the basic design that Melinda had originally put in. While that was happening, Melinda added on a renovation to her bathroom, as well as the one in Vivi's apartment. The elevator was installed in the garage, going up through a space made to accommodate it to the second floor. It opened onto a hallway that was made wide enough if walkers or wheelchairs were ever needed. The space did affect Vivi's apartment a little, but otherwise, everything was still intact. Vivi had indicated that her move to Stan's was complete, but it was always calming to her that in an emergency, she had a place to go.

Daniel started therapy. It was very difficult as it dredged up all his feelings about his father and the horrible way Michael had treated Melinda. Melinda was unaware that her kids were aware of Michael's infidelities. She thought she had spared them and saw no reason to bring it all up now. The truth was that whatever woman Michael was wooing often tried to get to the kids so that they would like her and give them favor in Michael's eyes. The barriers he was trying to break proved too difficult for him. Without telling Sarah, or anyone else, he stopped seeing the therapist.

He realized that his father's financial success was based on lies and deceit, but Michael presented himself with such assurance and confidence. Daniel so wanted to be that man that everyone looked up to. He got a high being the big guy in charge, even for the short time it lasted, and it was so difficult for him to relinquish it. He always admired Michael, always seemed to get what he wanted and be in control. Daniel loved that feeling that everyone was listening to him and that finally, he could call the shots. Finally, he thought he was in that position of power, only to have it crumble before him.

By the Spring, Sarah was pregnant. At first, all seemed well, but for Daniel, it was a nightmare. How would he ever be the hero in his child's eyes! He felt he had to start to do something quickly that would help him regain his feeling of superiority.

Melinda's new adventure was all set to go! Before the official launch of "Captain's Cookies and Melinda's Muffins," flyers were mailed out and signs posted. People in the area knew about the endeavor. The phone started ringing for orders and information. While the business could not handle a full commercial load, on the phone message and later on the webpage, it was clearly stated that supplies were limited and that all orders had to be placed at least two days before pickup. Tom even made a little roadside stand to handle the pickups. Manning the stand, a very friendly Hendricks, with his pitcher of sweet iced tea and his own supply of goodies, handled the business. On occasion, James would come to keep him company or give him a break. They had formed a little friendship that revolved around baked goods and baseball. Sometimes, especially on weekends, there were extra goodies that Melinda would mark down and sell it directly from the stand. Her best customers for these items, although it's a cliche, were the cops who patrolled the area. It was no surprise that they would get an extra or two, just for stopping by.

Life settled down for a while, and things were kind of predictable. The house for Sarah and Daniel finally got built. Daniel, Sarah and Steven, the newest member of the family, moved in. Although 3 million was a fortune for most people, Daniel thought of it as chump change. With "only" 3 million, he really had to be careful how he spent it. Scott and Dianna were right down the street, and over the hills, with Elizabeth and baby number 2 on the way. Tom and Melinda were so happy, often giggling like kids. She would do her baking, filling up the B&B with the most wonderful aromas. He would write when the spirit moved him, take care of his Captain business when necessary and lavish his attention on Elizabeth. Unity, true to form, was wherever Melinda was, except, of course, when James would be on the premises.

The next few years followed. Tom and Melinda made use of the city apartment, as well as the kids when business, school and time allowed. On this particular trip, Tom and Melinda were especially excited to see the opening of a Broadway show. The trip itself was noneventful, but the scheduled checkup at Tom's doctor was not. It was determined that Tom's cancer had come back. Although the radical surgery he had had was supposed to cure it, there is always a chance it would rear its ugly head again. It wasn't a death sentence, not by a long shot. It did mean that additional treatment was necessary and that the medical staff would come up with the treatment that made the most sense, considering the state of his health and his age. The rest of the time in the city was somber. Although the show was excellent, neither Tom nor Melinda could remember what it was about.

On the way home, Tom decided that he would have treatment in Virginia because he didn't want to be away from home. He would have his records transferred to an oncologist and urologist near home. The next night, Melinda asked everyone to stop over because there was some disturbing news to tell them. Tom told the story of his cancer and its recurrence. He emphasized that the doctor said it was treatable, but this might be the pattern of treatment and recurrence every few years. The good news, he said, was that new therapies are being discovered all the time, and he was very hopeful. The message was received but not believed. Yes, perhaps, there was a cure down the road, but in the meantime, they were worried about him and their mom as well. Tom began treatment within the week. In true Tom fashion, he did well, keeping a smile on his face. Melinda, of course, noticed that he held on to her a little more tightly and that there were times when she could hear him cry in the safety of his room.

CHAPTER FORTY-SIX

When Elizabeth was born, Tom started to use his talent for writing short stories and turned them into anthologies for children. The level of the stories he wrote corresponded to whatever age Elizabeth happened to be. He consistently read the stories to her. By the time she was 3, she had memorized so many of the stories that she could hold a book and pretend to read them while she recited from memory. She also, as soon as she was able, started to "illustrate" them. Tom delighted in the blobs of colors that she would present to him and would say proudly, "Look, Poppa Tom, it's the doggy from the story.!" He kept everything she drew and labeled it according to her wishes. By the time she was 6, her illustrations were easily recognizable, and Tom realized she had a talent for drawing. He encouraged her gift with ample books to illustrate and provided her with the art materials she needed. He got the idea to push the editor of his stories to create the books with the illustrations. The idea caught on before you knew it. A new phenomenon was created. The "What Have You Got To Say" series and illustrations hit the stands. Tom would create the story, Elizabeth would illustrate, and the rest of the family got to title each section. Almost everyone had fun, and the stories were so entertaining. The Titles of stories such as "What if the Flowers Were Stinky" or "The Day There Was No Pizza!" Tom was acutely aware that little Steven felt left out, so he made sure to find ways Steven could be a part of the action.

Daniel could only see this as a way Tom was trying to usurp his authority and power. Every time Steven mentioned Poppa Tom, Daniel's blood pressure would rise, and his anger would increase.

The pressure of fatherhood was now with Daniel, and he knew he should be enjoying this time of life. He wanted to call the shots; he wanted respect. He knew that he would never have the opportunity. He had become jealous of Tom. He wanted to be THAT man who had all the success and who everybody loved. Even with therapy he had, he started to slip back in equating control and success and his pay with his personal value. Most people would have been thrilled by his bankbook and his family as well. The long-awaited house was finally built, and it was lovely. Sarah had cut back on her hours in the dental practice to spend more time with the baby Steven, so the take-home pay was a little less. Still and all, his house was paid for, his Mom and Tom assumed the property taxes, and the future really seemed financially secure. He could just not get over that he felt demoted and relegated to an inferior position. Sarah was worried about the increasing depression she saw in him. He still carried the embarrassment of the scam because he saw how easily he could be manipulated when someone made him think he was in charge. He perceived Melinda as "still controlling the purse strings," and he felt stupid. He tried every day to just enjoy everything, especially Steven, but he felt angry all the time about most everything.

Dianna too had a very hard time accepting her role in the Will fiasco. She would berate herself about following orders that had no place in reality. Really!? A dead father instructing her to have her mother's house painted? If it weren't for Scott and the way he stepped up to help her through the whole incident, she would probably not have been able to handle it. The main difference between the siblings was that Dianna learned to immediately push the thought behind her whenever it reached her consciousness. She obviously would never forget it, and she would be on the lookout for things that sounded too easy or too wild. She realized what she did have, and she was comfortable with it. She didn't have to impress anybody.

Sarah's parents now had a very comfortable place to stay when they would visit. With a new grandchild, the visits became more frequent. As much as they enjoyed their home in Florida, they really enjoyed the Virginia time more. They felt so fortunate to be part of Steven's first three years.

On one morning, Sarah, her mom and dad (Phil and Judy) and Steven went on a little shopping trip to the outlets in Williamsburg. As much as the girls adored shopping, the boys did not! It became apparent that Granddad and Steven would much prefer to sit somewhere outside and never enter a shop. In order to let the women have their day, Phil and Steven strolled along the edge of the shopping plaza, stopping for an ice cream along the way and making a little trip to the toy shop. They spent about 3 hours in total. Steven was most definitely ready for a nap, and they started the hour trip back home.

When they arrived home, the toddler was fast asleep in his car seat. Sarah pressed the button in her car to open up the garage door. The most horrible sight greeted them. At first, she couldn't quite make out what she saw in front of her. Judy was facing backward, telling Phil to make sure he brought in all the packages. Then Sarah let out the most ungodly scream. Judy whipped around, and there it was, Daniel, hanging from the rafters. Steven awoke from the sound of his mother's scream. Grandpa quickly took the baby, not letting him see the sight before him. He felt that no matter how young Steven was, it would create an indelible impression in his brain. Tom and Melinda, who were in their home, heard the scream and ran out the front door. They saw Phil running with Steven towards them. Their first thought was something was wrong with the baby. All Phil could say was call 911, and he nearly collapsed with Steven in his arms. Melinda went back

136

into the house, grabbed her phone and ran out again and called 911. She just kept running to the garage where Tom was now getting Judy and Sarah out of the car and blocking the entrance to the garage. Melinda reached the garage as the operator asked her about the emergency. With the most horrified look on her face, and the inability to speak, she squealed, "He's hanging." Melinda fainted immediately.

Everything that followed was a blur to Melinda. Dianna, once again pregnant during an unspeakable tragedy, started to equate horrible things with her being pregnant. This would be the last child she vowed.

The men in the family, Tom and Scott, took over as the women could not. Charlene and Ken, Vivi and Stan helped with everything. James and Hendricks kept things functioning, the bakery business temporarily closed. Because of the well-known business, well-wishers hearing about the tragedy, left flowers, and signs and balloons out by the bakery stand alongside the road.

As his father before him, Daniel was cremated. Melinda kept the urn. She was unable to make peace with this for a very long time.

"Why?" was all Sarah could say. " He had everything. He had family, love, a beautiful home, money as well."

Charlene could only say, " It was a question of self-worth, and Michael apparently taught him that he wasn't worth the respect."

"My feelings are that I want to run away from this place. First, the ruination of my wedding and the cessation of Melinda's B&B, now depriving my son of his father. I want to run, but I feel paralyzed."

"You can't answer any questions quickly. Just remember that you were a wonderful, supportive wife and an attentive mother. None of what happened was your fault or your doing whatsoever. What you do from now on is totally up to you. I suggest you and Dianna and Melinda go somewhere for a few days and have a frank discussion. Go cry together, laugh together and see what is the path forward."

In the end, the three women did just that. What they decided would work for them even if everyone thought they were crazy.

CHAPTER FORTY-SEVEN

With all the frustrations Stan had in his life, the most difficult one for him was that Vivi would not marry him. Her divorce was now legally final, and she no longer had ties to Ari. Her children were grown with children of their own. Although they did communicate with Vivi, they were too bogged down in religious rhetoric and could not forgive their mother. Stan thought of a perfect solution. Without saying anything to Vivi, he went to a Conservative Rabbi and started the process of converting to Judaism. The Rabbi tried to dissuade Stan from the process, but Stan was relentless. The Rabbi eventually agreed because he knew that Aviva would continue to live with Stan. It was better if she did so with the sanctity of marriage. Finally, after the required amount of studies and the obligations of being converted, Stan became the first Wingate in his line of ancestors to claim the title of Jew! He was sure they were all turning in their graves, and if Mother were in her right mind, she would have apoplexy.

Vivi knew Stan was up to something; at first, she thought he was having an affair! She really couldn't accept or understand that, so she just waited until he was ready to tell her, no matter what was going on.

After work on a Friday afternoon, before Shabbos, Stan came home with his documentation, a Jewish star necklace around his neck, and a huge bouquet of flowers. He walked into the apartment and announced that he was a member of the Tribe! Vivi looked at him, took a long time to figure it out and just gasped. Stan got down on one knee, produced his mother's beautiful ring, which he had redesigned just for her, handed her the flowers and said, Aviva, will you marry me? I have tried everything I know to make you happy. Please be my wife?

Vivi looked at him, tears welling up in her eyes. " You converted for me?"
"Yes and no," he said. "I converted so that I would be part of who you are and because I love you so much. I converted to show you how much you mean to me. Please, Vivi, will you marry me?"

Vivi realized that anyone who would go through so much at this stage of life must truly be "beshert" for her. I would be honored to be your wife!"

It was all just really ritual. The marriage, the conversion didn't matter. It was just the symbolism. For the first time in each of their lives, they were whole. That night for the first time, Stan and Vivi went to synagogue for Shabbos. Needless to say, the Rabbi was shocked, thinking he would never see Stan again. Vivi was shocked, too, as an Orthodox Synagogue is quite different from a Conservative one. Vivi could handle it; good thing, she thought, he didn't go to a reform congregation.

CHAPTER FORTY-EIGHT

It was Tom's custom to go to the churchyard that contained the graves of his relatives ever since he came back to Richmond to liquidate his mother's house. He often pulled weeds, picked up twigs, and kept the headstones clean. He would bring flowers. While he was there one particular day, fresh from his diagnosis of the recurrence of his disease, he looked around for the first time and noticed the adjacent empty plot of land. He finished placing the flowers, said some prayers, and left the little graveyard. There were only a few other people laid to rest there that were not related to him. He walked through the adjacent property, then walked into the church looking for anyone who could possibly tell him who owned that land. The church was so small, and no one was there except for Sundays and Holidays. He scribbled a little note to the pastor, asking him to please call him about some business. That Monday, the pastor was eager to hear what Tom had to say and called him quite early in the morning. Tom asked him about the ownership of the adjacent lot and about the maintenance of the graveyard. The pastor gave him the necessary information but impressed upon Tom that it was a very poor church and had a tiny congregation. It was mostly the "old-timers" as he put it, who had been coming there all their lives. Children had moved away, just as Tom had done. The population had dwindled, and new churches with a more modern approach and outreach had taken hold of the people in the area. The church would function as a church as long as he would be there, but beyond that, he didn't know. Tom asked the pastor if he would be willing to change the focus of his church, and become a nondenominational house of prayer. If he could buy the lot next to the graveyard, he was willing to renovate the church building, keep up the current graveyard and build an atrium-type garden with niches for cremains . Since the people he was thinking about were from all different religions, it would have to be acceptable to whoever would choose to be interred there. He would set up a perpetual care for the graves and the garden that would fund the project for at least 100 years. The pastor would be called upon to run the funeral along with the wishes, as specific as they probably would be, and to allow clergy of a different faith to officiate if that's what the deceased had requested. He could continue to officiate at his church for as long as there was a congregation. Upon his retirement, there would be a management company who would take over the property, use the church for funerals, and manage the graves and cremains garden. The pastor asked about salary for his services and retirement benefits. A tentative plan was created if Tom could get the land and convince everyone to see and agree with his vision.

Tom knew as he drove back home that his extended family would all think he was depressed by his cancer setback, but he also realized that they all needed a plan because when someone would die, they would all run off in different directions. Just take the case of Michael. His cremains was somewhere in Daniel's house, probably in the attic or in a closet. Daniel's cremains was with Melinda! Tom felt that since death was inevitable, he wanted to take care of everything, so no one would have to be unprepared. Tom wanted to run through his idea with the family and friends.

He didn't want to call for "another serious" meeting, but he really felt that time was of the essence. When he got back home, he called everyone for a new project he was considering and requested their presence that evening. Although he tried to sound upbeat, the tone he conveyed was that something, again serious, had to be worked out. With trepidation, everyone gathered.

The tone of Tom's request concerned Melinda, but she decided to wait and find out what he had up his sleeve with everyone else. The "whole" clan meant Stan and Aviva, Charlene and Ken, Dianna and Scott, Phil and Judy, Sarah, and all grandchildren. It was an impromptu dinner, PIZZA! Always good, always fast and easy to clean up. After they had eaten, the grandkids were playing in a corner, and Unity was sitting at attention with Melinda. Tom spoke about his habit of going to the gravesites of his parents and siblings. This was common knowledge. He told them that he wanted to buy the adjacent parcel of land, which was totally empty, to create a niche wall garden. He described what he visioned and how he would be happy to fund the whole project. He cautioned that this was not a reaction to his latest health scare but something that was going to be down the road for all of them and that they should be prepared. He went into detail about the various religious backgrounds of the group and that it could accommodate both cremation and traditional burial. He spoke about the structure of perpetual funding.

There was silence from the adults. It took about a minute until Stan addressed the group and said.

"Tom, you're right; this is something no one wants to talk about or plan for until it's too late and someone dies and then you run around trying to make arrangements. I can tell you that Vivi and I have never discussed this. I guess we just never thought about it. I guess we would just go to the place our parents are without ever checking out if there was room for us or if we even wanted to be there. I think it's a great idea, certainly something to make grieving easier on all of us when the inevitable happens. I personally would rather be among friends, rather than relatives I hardly ever spoke to."

Reluctantly, each person contributed to the conversation. Perhaps, because of Vivi's background, she was stuck on being in a Jewish cemetery. Stan knew it would take some convincing, but she would come around. This was something to be mulled over, not a decision to come quickly. As if the air had been sucked out of the room, the flow quickly resumed to full blast, as people let the graveyard talk out of their minds and regained focus on the day at hand.

There was so much red tape, and it made Tom's head spin. He kept after all the details, had to revise some estimates, and had to follow laws of road setbacks and distances from property boundaries. It took six months to get this little project approved, which was much faster than most of these kinds of approval. Tom had to play his cancer card, hoping that he wasn't rushing to his own funeral. In the meantime, almost everyone came around to his way of thinking. The building of a columbarium has a lot of details, but the design is just a thing of choice. Not wanting a closed mausoleum, Tom, along with the construction company he chose, designed a free-flowing open-air design, where there were niches to be enclosed on the walls which would twist and turn, creating different gardens. People could visit the resting place of their loved ones while having the feeling of being in a pleasant garden and following a garden path. The feeling would be of open-air, but the angles of the walls would also create some covered areas so visitors could sit in the sun or shade. Each niche, or opening for an urn or box, would be sealed in the wall, and then the person's name and dates of birth and death would be inscribed. Tom pictured the old church, stripped down of religious symbolism, remodeled to contain comfortable chairs and a platform towards the far end that could serve as an altar, should someone request a formal funeral. Also, Tom wanted a book or books to contain something personal about the person who was laid to rest there. He envisioned everyone writing down a quick bio of themselves, just to declare that they were here and share a personal story. Nothing elaborate, unless they wanted that, but just a statement about their life. It wasn't a requirement, but Tom wanted more than just a name on a wall.

In the six months it took to get approval and then a year to become a reality, everyone warmed up to the idea. There were definite compromises on almost everything. The question arose about the empty places, either niche or grave, when the original group had gone to their resting places. Who would be allowed to occupy the empty spots? Of course, the grandchildren would have the spots bequeathed to them and their spouses and children. Eventually, there would be no spaces left. Tom could not look down the road that far. Way too many variables existed, but he did have an idea to continue it. He kept this to himself for the time being. It was finally decided that when the question came up for someone not in the official "family line" to request a spot, it would be decided by a board of directors who would hold the position for as long as they wished. The board was created to be Dianna and Scott, and Sarah. Little did they know how quickly their decision would have to be made.

Before completion of the project, Tom took the foreman of the project aside and asked for one little addition. In the rear of the property, but well within the property line, a miniature wall was created with approximately 24 little niches. In front of the wall, there were spaces for ten graves. All Tom wanted to be inscribed along the top of the wall was "In Loving Memory." Shortly after the columbarium was finished, Tom and Melinda got a call from VCU Hospital in Richmond. There was a man who came into the ER alone because he had the worst stomach ache in his life. When asked how long it had been going on, he told them probably five days or so. He was a wreck and afraid because he had been so healthy all of his life. By the time they got through all the paperwork and a scan, his appendix had apparently burst, and something as a simple appendix attack killed him. He had just waited too long. When he was asked for next of kin, the name he had provided was Melinda Radnor. The man was James. The committee had no problem accepting James to the family gravesite. The funeral home had a service, but only a few people came to pay their condolences. Hendricks did come, and he was visibly shaken. He informed Melinda and Tom that he was moving to South Carolina to be with kinfolk. He thanked them, Melinda, especially, for all the kindness she had given him over the years. The family grieved for James as if he were truly a member of their clan.

Shortly thereafter, age unknown, Unity passed away. It was as if she sensed that her buddy was gone. Unity occupies the space on that little back wall that Tom constructed for the family pets. Her picture and name are laminated on her closed niche.

Melinda was a wreck after Unity passed. She kept looking for that dog who followed her every move. Even with grandchildren running around, even with the chaos of the baking, there was a profound emptiness.

At this point, Melinda was ready to let go of Daniels' ashes. She felt it was time to take both the urns of Michael and Daniel and house them in the columbarium. Difficulty was in placing them in the wall. Did it really matter? She discussed it with the family, but most of all, Tom. She wanted to know if he wished to be next to Elizabeth in a grave or on the wall next to her. Tom had always assumed he would be buried next to Elizabeth, but now in this chapter of his life, he saw things differently. It was decided that Michael and Daniel would be placed on the top row of the eight levels next to each other. James had never expressed his desire to be cremated or buried. It was thought that he would have preferred burial, so he was placed with Tom's family in the old graveyard.

143

Tom chose cremation and wanted to be with Melinda. The two of them picked their desired location and then asked everyone else who wished to be cremated to select their spots as well. It was a bizarre conversation, no one likes to think about it, but this would save any conflicts in the future. Of course, there would be changes as families continued to grow and marriages took place, but at least it was a general plan.

Melinda held her special stone rolling it in her hands while she sat on her beloved patio. She asked and answered questions of herself and finally decided how to proceed. It was time to put Michael and Daniel in their final resting place. She stayed at the columbarium a long time until she was alone, and she spoke to them from her heart. "Michael, I have to forgive you. It was my fault that I put up with the life I had with you. I was not strong enough to stop the taunts and behavior that you exhibited. It was who you were, and I just got caught up in it. The blame is mine. I should not have let it continue for so long. I hope that there is something beyond this life and that you have found peace.

Daniel, my son. By the time you sought therapy after your father's death, I believe it was too late. I guess I was too wrapped up in my own life to see how your father's attitude and goals were impacting you. You were such a sweet child. You would chafe at your father pushing you and making you feel uncomfortable. I believe that's why you chose the work you did because you could meet those expectations easily but never clamored to go further. When the Will was read, you were thinking, and now you could finally be Dad. When the scam was exposed, you were devastated, not because you lost the money but because you lost the authority. I so wish you would have had help before the whole incident happened, but we can't go backward. I loved you unconditionally, as did Sarah. You will be forever missed. Your son, Steven, talks to you every day while looking at your picture. I forgive you for leaving us even though I will never understand it." It was a catharsis for Melinda. Now she would be able to remember them and even visit the cemetery without tears.

CHAPTER FORTY-NINE

When an outsider would look at Sarah, they would think she had a perfect life. She came from a loving family, they were well off, and she was well educated. She became a dentist, as was her father. She started off her professional career in his established office but didn't want to take over the practice when he retired. She was content working in another office where she was well received. She met Daniel and fell in love. Her family and his family meshed well, even though she thought her father-in-law was a bit overbearing and crass. Daniel didn't seem to have his father's ambition, but he wanted the respect it appeared his father commanded. He had gotten entrenched in his role in the business he entered after graduating college. He couldn't seem to extricate himself out of there. At first, he seemed content, and he made a very decent living, but he knew the job was a dead end with no possibility of further promotion. Since his parents were divorced, Sarah didn't get to meet his mother, Melinda, because she had moved to Virginia. The first time they would meet was a couple of days before they were to be married. She took a liking to Melinda immediately as well as Dianna, her sister-in-law.

What seemed like a fairy tale became a nightmare. The accidental death of her father-in-law, her husband's breakdown, the move to Virginia, the birth of her son, and her husband's suicide. Thank God for her parents and Melinda and Tom.

She was just getting back to herself. She had gotten a part-time job before Steven was born. She never went back after his birth, and with the subsequent death of Daniel, she had all but ceased to work. The pause became four years. It was time to resume her life. She, along with Dianna and Melinda, made the decision to stay in the home built for her and have her parents move in. Now she would gather herself, catch up with her profession and begin anew.

 She decided to go to a few lectures being presented on new techniques of procedures she had performed. The technology was new, and dental instruments, as well as better and stronger materials, were now available. One lecture featured a dentist named Rob Grant. When she entered the lecture room, she immediately noticed the tall, nice-looking black man towards the front of the room. As the room filled, he strolled up to the podium and introduced himself as Dr. Rob Grant. She listened attentively and wrote down many questions while he was talking. Since she had been out of the office for four years, she was not too surprised that much of it was new to her, but she was surprised that she had some difficulty following the lecture.   After he finished speaking and opened the floor to questions, she saw that the students in attendance seemed to follow the flow of conversations with far more clarity than she did. She decided to wait till the lecture was over to approach him. Sarah had always been a visual learner. She was disappointed that there hadn't been a video to accompany the lecture.

Dr. Grant had noticed the attractive woman take a seat while he spoke. She was older than the other students before him. He also noticed her attentively listening to the exchange of questions with a bewildered look on her face. He wondered why she hadn't asked anything. He didn't have to wait long as she approached him after the room cleared out. She introduced herself and said, " I was really interested in what you presented, but due to circumstances too long to explain, I have been out of the office for several years, and I was at a loss to visualize and understand a lot of the points you were making. " Do you have any literature on these procedures?"

"No, not with me, but I could certainly send some to you. You know what, I have finished here. I am starving. Why don't you come to lunch with me, and maybe I can help answer some of your questions and get your contact info so I can send you the literature."

"Oh please, Dr. Grant, I don't want to bother you and ruin your lunch."

Rob smiled and said, " First, call me Rob. Second, It would be a pleasure. Now don't deny me your company, I promise to behave. Your name again?

Sarah sizing up the situation, said," My name is Sarah, and I really want to know what you were talking about. I am trying very hard to get back into dentistry after a terrible few years."

Rob didn't know if she was serious, had she really gone through troubling times, or was she just trying to gain his attention. "If you want me to be coherent, I really have to eat something. I tend to be hypoglycemic, and I get hangry! "Hangry?" Sarah inquired. "Yup, hungry and angry." Sarah smiled. "Okay," she said, "I wouldn't want to see you hangry!"

Sarah and Rob walked down the street from the lecture hall to a hamburger joint where Rob ordered a huge lunch. Sarah was starting to really feel uncomfortable and ordered an iced tea. Normally, this place had fast service, and today was an exception. The food was taking forever, or at least that's the way Rob felt. They had some small talk, and it was obvious that Rob was getting agitated.

Rob was starting to size up this woman sitting across from him in the booth. She seemed nervous, and she didn't say where she had worked. Finally, Sarah questioned several points of the procedure that had been eliminated. She was concerned that this would lead to a poor long-term result. This angered Rob because he felt that Sarah was trying to discredit his lecture. He had an experience like this before where some woman was just coming on to him. " I'm trying to figure out what is going on here. Are you even a dentist? Rob started sweating and started saying insulting things and raising his voice. He yelled something about women; Sarah recognized that he was having a serious hypoglycemic episode. She quickly called over a waitress and yelled at her to get a Coke fast. Rob started yelling, too, as nausea started to hit him. "What, are you an MD too? I know how to take care of myself.

The Coke arrived, and Sarah just barked the order for him to drink. He drained the glass, and within a few minutes, he was starting to feel better. Sarah asked, "When was the last time you had eaten? Maybe you should keep some glucose tablets with you."

Rob responded angrily from embarrassment, and he knew he was being stupidly defensive. Sarah had had enough as he couldn't seem to recover himself. She got up from the booth, looked at him before leaving and said, "You are an ass. You feel so high and mighty that you can't accept my help. Is that because I am a woman or because I questioned your expertise? You want to know who I am and why I am here? I came to show my ignorance and question my past experience. Isn't that what everyone does when they are trying to re-enter their professional field? Maybe you thought I was trolling for a boyfriend or a husband. Sure, that would make husband number three because husband number 2 committed suicide, and that was after his Father killed himself the day after our wedding. My son, who barely remembers his father, would really be in need of a male figure, so I guess I planned this as a way to get one for him. Have a nice lunch."

Dr. Robert Grant had really screwed up. Sarah was now resigned to the fact that no matter what she did, everything would always come out wrong. She was so angry and hurt, she couldn't think.

A lady sitting at a nearby booth had overheard the conversation. She went over to Rob to rub a little salt in the wound. "Hey, you'd better make that right because you were way out of line. You just did what other people have done to me, make assumptions without any knowledge."

Rob knew she was right. He could rationalize it away saying that he was having a hypoglycemic episode but he knew that wasn't true. His reaction was way more, it frightened him but he didn't know why. He liked giving these lectures, watching the eager young dentists flock around him, making him feel like he was the boss! Sarah didn't fit the picture, she was a little withdrawn and more mature. Was it true what she said? He should never have questioned her credentials or dismissed her questions. Yea, she was right, he was too full of himself. He quickly swallowed a few bites of his

147

burger, had the rest wrapped to go. He had stopped sweating and the nausea had abated. He hoped to find Sarah before she drove home, wherever that was.

Sarah had walked outside and was completely confused as to where her car was parked. She tried to collect herself, but she just couldn't think straight. She got back to the parking lot, found her car. The tears started streaming down her face. She was so distracted as she pulled out of the parking space that she backed up into a car that was passing at that second. It was quite a bang, she knew that there was damage to both vehicles. She managed to turn off the car, get out and inquire if everyone was OK. Everyone was not. Nothing serious, but nevertheless required attention. She had just had it. Right before she passed out she remembers seeing Rob Grant's face in front of her.

Sarah wasn't out for long. It was the consequence of Rob's attitude, enduring depression, lack of food, and shock of the accident. She was on a gurney in an ambulance that was still in the lot. There were police and a small crowd. She immediately remembered everything that had preceded the accident. While she knew she couldn't drive, she refused to go to the hospital. She would leave her car in the spot and take an uber home. The people in the other car were shaken up as well, some minor abrasions and a very dented car. The parties involved gave the police their report. Sarah took total responsibility and assured the occupants of the other car that she would cover anything not allowed by insurance. Papers were exchanged, the police report filed and the scene cleared out. Rob had been sitting in his car waiting for all the activity to die down. He watched to make sure that Sarah was not seriously hurt, and concerned about how she would get home. When it appeared that Sarah was ready to leave he drove over to her and asked her to please let him take her home. He told her he was sure that he was truly the cause of the accident and that he just felt awful and knew he could not make up for what he had put her through. Sarah totally agreed with him. In spite of her previous encounter with him, she agreed to the ride. She felt it was the least he could do.

On the way home, Sarah was just spent. She finally spoke, " My name is Dr. Sarah Radnor, and indeed I am a dentist. Everything I said to you was 100% true. I finally decided a couple of weeks ago that my mourning was over and it was time to get back on my own two feet. I had the luxury these last 4 years to try and heal. Both my Parents and my Mother in-law nurtured me and got me through the nightmare that still haunts me. I truly thought that I was doing a responsible thing by catching up on my skills. I know I am rusty and that there is a lot that has taken place since I was practicing at the office. I had no idea who was giving the lecture, I chose that particular class because of the topic. I didn't care if you were male or female, if you were a black man or blonde and blue eyed. I was only interested in your expertise. I was not trolling for a man, and most assuredly not for a husband. If it was as simple as that, I would have accomplished that already."

Rob knew he deserved the talking down to. "I profusely apologize. I told you I get weird when I haven't eaten, and if you allow I will use that as my excuse, because honestly, it was inexcusable. Please let me make amends. I have several interesting patients next Wednesday, one is a dental implant, that procedure we were discussing. Please come to the office and either observe or assist, ask all the questions you want. I can send a car for you if you don't have a way to get there."

Sarah at first wanted to refuse, but she thought perhaps this incident could have a silver lining.

"Ok, what time and the address please. I can get there myself."

He told her he would text the office location to her. When they got back to the B&B, he took down her number. She started to exit her car, but she got a little lightheaded and unsteady. Melinda had seen the car pull into the driveway and then watched as Sarah seemed in distress. Melinda immediately went outside and got to the car as Rob was helping Sarah to her feet.

" It's OK, I'll explain. Where are my Parents?" Sarah didn't really want anyone to see her like this, but she was thankful for Melinda's help. Melinda didn't know what to make of Sarah coming home in a strange car and watching Rob seem to fret over her.

" They went out shopping, Sarah, are you OK?" She looked at Rob, inquired as to who he was and questioned him as to why he was driving her home and why she seemed out of it.

Rob introduced himself and explained that she had a little fender bender that he caused and he drove her home because she was too shaken up to drive safely. Melinda assumed he and Sarah had somehow collided in their cars, but his car was untouched. She thanked him for bringing her home and then quickly got Sarah into the house.

Melinda was curious as to what happened, but Sarah had no intentions of telling her. She needed to eat something and get herself together. The texted information came and Sarah was set to go and watch Dr. Rob work. Sarah felt confused as well. Did she accept his invitation because she saw a way to learn and advance her career, or was she somehow attracted to him. Maybe she should have just left it at calling him an ass!

Later that day, Steven was waiting for his Mom to have dinner. He was all smiles as the macaroni and cheese was before him. He told Sarah all about his day at school and had an even bigger grin when one of Momma Melinda's cookies was dessert. He also told Sarah that these were his favorite cookies because he helped make them. He cracked the eggs into the batter all by himself, and he was very proud.

CHAPTER FIFTY

Elizabeth had grown into a lovely young woman. She was a child of privilege and she knew it. While she heard the anguish and struggles of her family, she was hardly ever touched by it. She knew the stories concerning her Grandfather, the inheritance and she remembered the suicide of her Uncle, but she was sheltered from it by her Parents, her Grandmother and Poppa Tom. She was also surrounded by an artificial extended family of Momma Melinda's friends , the people who worked at the B&B and Sarah's Parents. In their attempt to protect her, they denied her a chance to learn what the real world was like. She lived in a crystal bubble, which was later extended to include her siblings and cousins.

Elizabeth had a talent in drawing. She had exhibited at an early age that she could put down on paper things she saw. Dianna and Scott were blown away, because neither one of them could make a straight line. When Elizabeth started illustrating Tom's stories, everyone realized she had an exceptional talent. When she started looking at Colleges and Universities, she was confused as to what the major focus of her education should be. Her choices were unlimited, but she decided to stay close to home. Virginia Commonwealth University had a fine Art department. While she definitely had a preference for drawing she wanted to learn how to work with other art media   as well. She was particularly drawn to the French school of Art, from the classical to the impressionists. She decided to take advantage of a program at VCU that would let her take courses in Paris. Elizabeth did not have an ear for language. She tried valiantly, but could only manage very basic conversation for all of her studies.

Poppa Tom had doted on Elizabeth from the day she was born. She was for him everything he had wanted in his life, and could never attain for himself. The child that he would love and nurture. He did not usurp the job of parenting, but was more like a fairy Godfather, that was there to grant her more outrageous wishes while watching over and protecting her. He thought about his deceased wife Elizabeth, and the woman she might have become had she lived beyond her early 20's. While she was the quintessential model, his Goddaughter had a more subtle beauty and intelligence and intellectual drive. She was a hard worker and had found something to stir her passion that she could turn into a lifelong body of work.

Socially, Elizabeth was awkward. While she had a large group of general friends, she had no best friend. There was no mention of a boyfriend, or even an acknowledgement that someone was "cute". Apparently, as her friends had started to pair off, she often felt left out. For a while after High School graduation, she felt better, her High School friends were scattered around the country and she was preparing for her future. Once again, she had difficulty connecting to people she was meeting. That was when it dawned on Elizabeth that she was "different."

She didn't think anything was particularly wrong except she couldn't get caught up in her friend's social activities. She decided to talk to Poppa Tom about it. When she asked him to go somewhere to talk, he didn't flinch. She had often done that and felt that it was their special connection with which they were both so comfortable.

Tom wanted to buy some new clothes for Elizabeth and her upcoming trip to Paris. She happily accepted his offer to go shopping and was pleased that now, she could drive him wherever they decided to go. She parked the car at the mall and Elizabeth just started talking.

"Poppa, something is wrong with me. I have friends both boys and girls. In the last year or so, many, well most have kind of separated into couples. We're still friends, but it's starting to feel odd. I just don't feel any attraction to anyone. I don't get it, I have no attraction to boys or girls. At first I thought I was gay, but that's not the case. Why doesn't anyone excite me? I must send out vibes cause no one comes over to me either.

"Sweetheart, I think it just might be that you haven't met the right people yet. I'm not sure I am the one to speak to. This is way outside of my experience. You realize, I have never been a young woman! I understand your worry, I am just not sure you should worry."

"Poppa, it's really bothering me, I think I'm friendly, I just don't find anyone interesting!

"I can help you find help, let me research it a little, but I want you to know that no matter what you learn about yourself, it is OK. "

"Well, of course you would say that," she said with a smile, "You love me, I just don't want to ever disappoint you."

"You never could," came the answer.

The two of them got out of the car and entered the store. Elizabeth chose about a dozen outfits. Some were outrageous, she tried them all on to give Tom the giggles. When she finally finished, she chose most of the things she tried on! Just as they were leaving the store, they overheard the cashier say to the next customer, "Hey, wasn't that Captain Cookie?" They both burst into laughter.

"I have been thinking." Tom said, " I want to take you to Paris and get you set up. I think that you will be more comfortable in a little apartment near the Art Institute than in a dorm like situation. Maybe something alone or with a roommate. I know Paris very well, and have a connection or two.

152

Can I come with you, just to get you settled, or is that too much and I will cramp your style."

Elizabeth was thrilled with the idea. "Poppa", she said, "It isn't too much on your health, is it?"

"I will be fine, I am doing very well." Tom knew he had lost weight and was looking a little frail, but in all honesty, he felt good!

CHAPTER FIFTY-ONE

Sarah walked into Dr. Rob Grant's office fifteen minutes early. She wanted a chance to get oriented to the procedure room and dental tools that would be used. She greeted the staff, announced who she was and was escorted into Rob's office. He was seated at his desk and stood up as she entered.

" I am really delighted you came today, there is space in that closet," he said pointing to the one closet in the room, " leave your purse or whatever there and let me show you around the office."

It was well appointed, with the latest in equipment and what seemed to be a friendly staff. There were 4 treatment rooms, two where dental hygienists worked and two rooms reserved for procedures. The waiting room looked comfortable, with an accessible powder room. The office staff had a T shaped area with a private area for financial transactions, and two spaces for checking people out and making new appointments. The reception area which was open to the waiting area had glass partitions that seemed to remain open while someone was in the office. There was another powder room in the hallway between exam rooms and Rob's private office which was the size of an average bedroom. It contained shelves with many books, a desk, a loveseat, and two chairs. The walls were adorned with diplomas, and other testimonials. There were no photos or pictures of family that Sarah noticed.

Rob introduced her to the staff, making sure to call her Dr. Radnor. Sarah asked that she be called Dr. Sarah instead.

Finally Rob and Sarah went into the procedure room where he showed her the materials and tools that would be used with the upcoming patient. She looked things over and asked about some tools that she had used previously and was told that the new method streamlined the procedure and eliminated several steps she had used before. She inquired about types of anaesthetic injections he used, did he feel the need for something like nitrous oxide or if at any time consider an IV sedation. He was pleased that she had a wide range of knowledge. Finally the patient arrived, introductions made. Rob was impressed with the easy way Sarah had around this patient. Her presence helped the patient to relax. The procedure went smoothly and the time flew by for Sarah. She only had one complaint that she didn't share with anyone. Rob was a great deal taller than Sarah, and she found herself standing on her toes to see what was taking place in the patient's mouth. The height of the dental chair was a little too high for her. Nevertheless, she was able to get everything that was going on and was impressed with how this particular method of treatment cut almost 40 minutes off the previous way. The results too, were statistically better. When the patient was finished, there was a 20 minute gap, till the next patient. Rob and Sarah reviewed all the steps and she was satisfied she understood it perfectly.

The next patient to arrive was there for a routine cleaning and exam. The hygienist placed the man in the room. He was a difficult patient from the standpoint that he had neglected his teeth for so long and knew that he was in for a lot of pain. The very competent woman trying to deal with him was having difficulty just getting him comfortable in the chair.

Hearing the ruckus, Sarah asked Rob if she could go in and calm him down. He thought, why not! Sarah looked forward to the challenge, she walked in with a big smile on her face and told him that he had just won the dental lottery.

"What! You mean I can go home?"

Sarah looked at him and said, "Sure you can go home, right after I give you one of the most painless exams you ever had!"

He laughed and said, "Lady, if you can do that, I will be your patient for life,"

She chuckled and had the hygienist put the towel around his neck. At first glance into this very poorly neglected mouth, she knew that there would be pain. " You know what, I bet you have pain without anyone touching your mouth. I rescind my offer, but I will promise you this, if you let me take care of this, and it will take time, the pain you constantly have will be gone, and I will be a heroine. "

"OK sweetheart he said, and if I can chew a steak without crying, I will take you out for dinner!"

"Deal!" she said, and the exam before the cleaning started. Sarah asked the man if he had any asthma or lung problems. When he said no, she suggested they try nitrous oxide, better known as laughing gas. She explained how it worked and he agreed. She prepared him for the sensation the gas would cause and saw when he seemed calm and comfortable. Even with the gas, he winced a little, but Sarah's manner and resolve got the exam over without much complaint. She stayed with him until the nitrous oxide was out of his system.

Rob entered the room and his patient looked at him and said, "You better keep this one here doc, cause she is my personal dentist from now on! Remember, steak will be on me whenever this mess turns back into a mouth!" She handed his chart to Rob and let him create a schedule for the work Mr. Williams would need.

Sarah stayed for the rest of the appointments of the day. She was exhilarated and Rob was impressed. The patient's loved her, the staff worked well with her. She walked back into the office room after everyone except she and Rob left. She plopped down, exhausted, on the love seat. Rob sat in a chair opposite her.

"That was nice work today, it makes me feel more like an ass than I already did. You know it is going to take the rest of my life to apologize to you."

"You know, I think it will," she said with a wink. "I enjoyed my day, I thank you for it. I realize that 4 years is a huge amount of time to miss out on changes. I think that I can come back into the workforce as long as I have a mentor to keep teaching me so I can get up to date."

"So come work here, if you don't, Mr. Williams will follow you wherever you go!"

Sarah thought about what she was going to say. She was disturbed that she found him so attractive and she honestly wanted to be around him.

"Sure, I can work here, but under my terms, which you can assume are numerous,"

Rob wasn't sure if she was serious or not. "OK let's hear these terms. Honestly, number one. If I have a complaint, or you have a complaint, let's get it out in the open immediately. If at any point we find we cannot work together, then I leave, no drama, no fight. Number 2, I am a Mother, my child comes first over anything. I am fortunate that I have childcare. But in any emergency, if Steven needs me I am there. Number 3 If you get hungry you better eat something right away because I will never be subjected to one of your tirades again. Number 4 is an immediate thing, the height of the dental chairs is too high for me, I have been stretching all day and my neck is sore. Do you have any Advil?

"No, but I have some BioFreeze, it's a role on, that should help. Why didn't you say anything?" He reached into his desk drawer and withdrew the bottle. "I just thought I could compensate for the height difference, I didn't think I was going to hurt so much."

Rob hesitated for a minute. "Here it is, handing the bottle to her." Sarah looked at it and asked if he could apply it as she thought she wouldn't be able to reach all the spots that were hurting.

"I am afraid to touch you," was his answer.

Sarah said, "OK this is not a test. I know how to say no if things get weird. You can start your life long apology to me now. My neck is sore and then you can show me how to get those chairs to a lower level."

Sarah moved over on the love seat to make room for Rob. Reluctantly he came over and started to apply the lotion. It felt good, too good. She was trying so hard to stay quiet but she started to moan as softly as possible. Rob's hands started to move down her spine. His fingers hitting all those sore spots. Finally with his hands still on her back he asked her, " Is this OK, should I stop."

156

Sarah answered, " You can stop when you feel you should or when I say no, whichever comes first."

Rob said to her, "You know there is a strong attraction here, but I don't want to emphasize it or rush it. I'm walking on eggshells here."

Sarah was surprised when he lifted his hands from her body. She turned her around to face him , looked directly into his eyes and said, " I don't want you to stop, but you are right. This is way too fast. I am just on a high from today, and it feels so good. I realize that I could jeopardize working here, but let me understand if I am reading the attraction wrong. I know we both take risks.

After a brief moment of silence, Sarah decided to break the deadlock. "Do you need assurances from me? You already know that I am a damn good dentist and that what I was saying about my absence from work was true. I am so very tired Rob, I don't want to work this hard when I find someone attractive to me and who speaks my language and shares my professional goals. This is me. My body aches today, but my mind aches from life. If you are hesitant, I can wait. Just don't make me wait too long."

Sarah couldn't believe that she was pushing Rob to be intimate with her. She knew that she was so hungry for his touch. This just wasn't like her. She was always the "good" girl who played by the rules, and here she was creating the rules. She was so desirous of his touch.

Rob honesty wasn't sure what he felt, but here she was right in front of him and he was so attracted to her. He didn't say a word, he just kissed her, a long passionate kiss. Still there was something holding Rob back. Sarah took out her phone, called her Mom and said she would be there for dinner, make sure Steven practiced his reading and that she would take him for frozen custard for dessert.

He was hesitating, but why? If he tried to think this out then the opportunity would be lost and might not come again. He just didn't want it to end badly. He told her to wait and he would add a little more lotion to her neck. The lotion went on cold which caused her to gasp and goosebumps appeared on her upper arms. Rob put down the lotion and placed his hands over the bumps to gently massage them away. Tension was building up between them and his hands started to go down her arms caressing them. She turned towards him, trying to read his eyes. "Are you sure?" she asked. He just continued to rub up and down her arms. She reached over for her purse, grabbed her phone and dialed her Mom. "Something has just come up," she said, "tell Steven I will be about an hour late but we will definitely get frozen custard." She put her phone down, stood up and asked him again, " are you sure?" He needed no more encouragement. It was true the office was not a comfortable place to make love, but it was so intense that neither of them cared. There were so many new sensations and observations for the two of them. Neither had ever been with a person not of their own race. The contrast of their skins was an aphrodisiac. Each of them was so hungry for release that they finished way too quickly. Because Sarah had made the date with her son, there wasn't enough time for an encore. Almost as an afterthought, she was aware that Rob had used a condom. He looked at it while taking it off and saw that it had been ruptured. He didn't tell her. It haunted him because he wasn't telling a lie, he was just not announcing the truth. They hurriedly dressed, calmed down and just kissed a little more, but she had to go. It would feel odd over the next few days to pretend like it didn't happen, try to fool the staff that nothing was between them, and try to make time for it to happen again.   They would pretend at the end of the day to say goodby and then each would drive the short distance to Rob's house. Like all new relationships, the intensity is high, the sex abundant, and the little things that annoy are placed way in the rear. The discovery between the two of them was exciting and life changing.

Sarah had told her family all about the Practice and Rob. She told them that they were going to try dating and see what happened. Sarah had never dated a black man before, and her parents did have concerns. They put those on the back burner, and welcomed Rob to their home when he came to visit, about two weeks later.   Steven had been waiting patiently and he had a burning question to ask Rob. Since his Dad's death, Steven had taken to looking at photo albums, including the wedding photos taken at the B&B. He waited for Rob to sit and talk with him a while and then whipped out the photo of James at the wedding. Steven asked Rob if Mr. James was his brother. Rob was surprised to see the photo, he had no idea who Mr. James was, and he said to Steven, "No, Mr. James and I are not related, I am just another Black man." Steven had his curiosity satisfied, no further questions asked.The two of them did talk for quite a while and Rob asked him if he had ever been to the Children's Museum in Richmond. When Steven said no, Rob asked if he would like to go because they had some really cool hands on exhibits for kids his age. Sarah thought it was a good idea, she wanted Steven to get to know Rob and feel comfortable around him.

Sarah's parents were nervous about the proposed outing. There are a lot of crazy people out there, what if they think that Steven is not with Rob voluntarily. What if someone tries to take Steven because they think they would be protecting him. What if….. What ifff?

Mom, Dad, I know your heart is in the right place, but do you think I would ever put Steven in harm's way? This is part of the problem with racism. Rob and I have discussed it, hell we have even lived it. When we first met we had a bit of this too between us! Steven wants to go, he is comfortable with it and so am I. Rob and I have become very close over the last few weeks. After what happened, I can breathe again. Get used to Rob being around, I think it's going to be permanent. Phil and Judy were uncomfortable with it, but they were trying to let her know that if that was her decision they would deal with it.

Nine weeks later ,Sarah came to work very distracted. She greeted the staff, and went right to Rob's office. He was sitting behind his desk at the computer. She closed the door behind her, and sat down in one of the chairs.

"Rob, I don't know how to say this, and I don't know how this happened, but I'm pregnant!" You know I didn't plan it or try to entrap you!

Rob's head snapped up like someone had just hit him hard. Before he could respond, he knew exactly how it happened. Why had he not told her about the condom!

"Say something please, I want to figure this out together." She looked at him pleadingly.

Rob started, "Oh Sarah, I am such a jerk. I know how this happened. I was so sure nothing would, I never mentioned it to you."

"What the hell are you talking about?" she realized she spoke too loudly.

"Our very first time together, right here, I noticed when I took the condom off, it was ruptured. I was going to tell you but I didn't want to ruin that first experience. I was so sure nothing bad would result from it. But Sarah, is this something bad? He got up, walked around the desk and crouched down at the chair she was sitting in.

"You and I are not kids, I never had the hope in my head of being a father. Marry me Sarah. It would make me the happiest man on earth, if you and Steven became my family. It's ridiculous I know that after 2 months I know that you are who I want to spend my life with. Please, Sarah, be my wife.

Sarah's head was swimming with emotions and her body with a good deal of nausea. She was trying to keep everything under control.

"You're happy?" she asked.

"Answer the question", he said, "then I will know how I feel".

Sarah was still in a fog. "You want me AND the baby?"

" Wait! Would you be asking me this if I wasn't pregnant? All of a sudden this comes out of your mouth?

Rob walked around the desk to the chair.

"I was trying to think of a way to ask, and yes it's all I have thought about. I thought it would be too soon for you. Sarah, will you marry me?"

"Rob, you barely know anything about me! You don't even know if I have a religion, or if I snore!"

"Sarah, I know what I have to know, everything else can be worked out, well maybe not the snoring! Sarah, will you marry me?"

"Yes yes I will." She got up from the chair, walked right past Rob holding out his arms to her, and ran to the bathroom and promptly vomited.

About 15 minutes later they were laughing, knowing that what had happened had to rate as the most unromantic proposal and acceptance ever.

Six weeks later, Rob and Sarah were married. The wedding consisted of the people in Sarah's life, and Rob's two brothers and their families who lived in Richmond. The two were married in Charlene's Church. They wrote their own vows, and promised to never let Rob get hangry!

Steven, holding Rob's hand as they walked out of the Church, told him he could not call him Dad, because he had a Dad. Rob said that was ok but what would he call him? Steven thought about it and said, You will be my Poppa Rob, and just like that, it was decided.

Just short of eight months later, twin boys were born to Mom and Poppa. Steven was so thrilled to be a big brother. Two years later a baby sister was born to complete the family.

Judy and Phil had moved out of the house right before their daughter got married, as it was just too uncomfortable for Rob to be under a microscope. It was the best thing to do. They found an adorable 55+ community close by so they were still available along with Melinda and Tom for babysitting and grandparent loving.

CHAPTER FIFTY-TWO

Elizabeth could barely believe that she was on her way to Paris! Luckily she knew two other students who were going to be there as well. They decided if they couldn't find lodging together, they would at least live near each other. Since neither of the other students were studying art, it just wouldn't work out that they could spend too much time together. Nevertheless, it would be comforting to know someone in the city. Tom was totally uncomfortable with Elizabeth doing this virtually alone but he had to realize that she was ready to be on her own. Dianna and Scott tried to talk him out of doing everything for her. She had to spread her wings, but Tom just wanted to get her settled.

He had been to Paris many times in the past, and was giggling as Elizabeth was oohhing and ahhing as the taxi made its way from the airport to the city. To Elizabeth it was magical. Tom had them checked into a hotel that offered two rooms. He insisted that she call him Dad for the trip just so they wouldn't raise any eyebrows.

First order of business was for Elizabeth to check into the art facility which she did the very first day. In the meantime, Tom said he was checking out some rentals .

" Puis-je vous aider?" asked the young man at the desk.
Immediately flustered, Elizabeth stuttered and finally said, "Sorry, I speak very little French!"
The young man smiled and asked in English, "Well, then how do you expect to learn anything here?"

She couldn't come up with an answer and he finally said, "Take it easy, I was just teasing you. Can I have your name and why you're here?"
Elizabeth relaxed and gave him the information.
"Listen," he said, "You will be fine, but perhaps you need a friend. I'm Charlie. I'm a photojournalist student, this is my 3rd year. Did you just arrive?"
"Yes, and already I am flustered. I'm just here for the year, my genre is drawing, although sometimes I paint as well."
" Do you go by Elizabeth or Liz or something else?"
"You know no one has ever asked me that before. What do I look like to you?"
" To me you are Eliza! Can I call you that?"
"Why not, here is to new beginnings."

Charlie helped her fill in the forms that needed information and he asked her where she was living. When she said her Father was out looking for a place right now, he asked her if she was willing to share an apartment with him as his roommate had just graduated and moved on. He said he could show her the apartment later in the day and have her Dad come and check it out. He gave her the information and told her to drop by at 3PM..

She knew that this would be too much for Poppa, but she thought it would be fun!

Elizabeth texted Tom and told him to just check out the location while he was out and about.

When Tom and Elizabeth both got back to the hotel, Tom was in full "DAD" mode.

"Who is this guy? How did he know you were looking for a place? I don't like it!"

Elizabeth laughed and said, "Really! Good thing you didn't know half the stuff I did in school right under your nose!"

Tom got a hold of himself. Oh my, she had grown up and he never saw it happen.

Later that day, at 3pm they stood at the entrance to Charlie's apartment. Much to Tom's chagrin, it was a nice building in a nice area and very close to school. They rang the bell, opened the street door when the buzzer let them in and climbed 3 flights of stairs. Charlie was waiting for them at the apartment door.

"Bon jour," He greeted them. To everyone's surprise, especially Elizabeth, Tom spoke in fluent French.

"Bon jour. Elle n'a aucune idee je parle francais. Je suis son parrain, et c'est mieux d'etre legitime." (She has no idea I speak French. I am her Godfather and this better be legitimate.)

Both Charlie and Elizabeth stood there with mouths hanging open.

"Poppa Tom! Really! You didn't think that it was a good idea to tell me you spoke French?"

Charlie could only answer, "Yes Sir, this is legitimate."

He showed them the apartment, especially that the two bedrooms were separated by a living room and kitchen. There was only one bathroom. The bedroom was empty except for a bed and dresser.

"I'm afraid that is all there is, my last roommate took everything else with him.

"How much is the rent? I wasn't expecting Paris to be quite as expensive as it seems to be." Elizabeth really had no idea what was expensive and what wasn't!

162

"I have to check with the landlord. She said that there would be a rate change after my roommate left. I can tell you it is very competitive with other apartments in this area."

Tom thought that this was very peculiar, "I would think you would know immediately what the rent is? There is something I don't like here. I also don't think I like the idea of you, Elizabeth sharing an apartment with this person. I have seen enough. As you keep telling me, you are an adult now, so I will wait for you downstairs in the lobby and you make up your mind!"

Tom immediately left the apartment. Elizabeth and Charlie just stood there. Finally Elizabeth spoke. "I really do like the apartment, especially what would be my room. It is filled with light and it would be a good studio for me. I don't know what to say about my Godfather. I have never seen him like this. What are you thinking Charlie? Is Poppa Tom too much, he will be going home you know."

"I think if you stay here and you get a splinter, he will come here as soon as he can and beat me up! Wow, was he always so protective?"

While the two of them tried to figure out the situation, Tom walked down to the lobby almost laughing. He knew that if Elizabeth took this apartment, Charlie would be on his best behavior. As he amused himself with the thought, a woman entered the building, looked up at him and said, "Mon Dieu, Thomas,   est-ce que c'est toi? (Is that you?)

Tom looked up from his private thoughts and faced Marie Claire. "Marie Claire, Que faites-vous ici?" (What are you doing here?)

Marie Claire smiled and said, "This is my building, remember, I gave you the address only last week! I was expecting to be in touch tomorrow!"

Tom quickly checked the address. Strange that when Elizabeth told him where they were going he hadn't realized that building was his destination after all!

" Oh no! I think I may have screwed up. But come here and give me a hug, it's been ages.!"

Marie Claire laughed and gave him a huge hug. "I have a feeling something unexpected has happened? Where is your Goddaughter?"

She is upstairs looking at an apartment with this young man who needs a roommate. I may have been a little hard on him?"

"Apartment 4 H?" she asked.

"Why yes, who is he?"

Marie Claire started to laugh. She didn't answer, she just started walking up the steps. Tom followed.

At the landing for the 4th floor, Marie Claire walked to apartment 4 H, knocked on the door and walked in. Tom stood behind her.

"Charlie, I see you have a new roommate?"

"Bon jour, Meme. This is a friend I just met at the Institute, Elizabeth, this is my Grandmother."

Elizabeth greeted Marie Claire and then saw Tom standing in the doorway. Not knowing at all what was going on, Elizabeth was shocked as Marie Claire walked over to her and gave her a huge hug.

Tom saw all the confusion and intervened. " Elizabeth, this isn't exactly as I planned, but Marie Claire was your namesake's best friend. We have kept in touch all these years.

Marie Claire then introduced her Grandson by saying, "I guess you and Charlie have already met."

"Poppa? What is this?"

Tom walked in and sat down on a couch. "Ok, When you chose to come to Paris, your Grandmother had me call Marie Claire to see if she might know of a nice apartment you could use while you were here. She said, yes, she had a perfect place near the Institute. She didn't tell me that her Grandson also lived in the building. I was going to surprise you that I found a great place and then let you in on the whole story, but you met Charlie first! I spoke to Marie Claire yesterday.

" I am quite angry right now. I thank you for always looking out for me, but I would very much like to start making my own decisions. Madam, thank you for trying to help, but I can't share this apartment with Charlie, too much of a set up. You're off the hook Charlie, you won't have to babysit me."

"Marie Claire continued, "Elizabeth, no this was not the apartment! The one I was keeping for you is 4J. It is a one bedroom, very sweet. Come look at it." Marie Claire walked out of the apartment and everyone followed.

Elizabeth was shown an adorable, but very small apartment. It was basically a tiny kitchen, with a sitting area, a bathroom and a bedroom. It was more than enough but it was tight, and Elizabeth could not figure out where she could set up her art materials. As if he read her mind, Charlie whispered something to her. She and Charlie excused themselves and went into the little bedroom. They came out a few moments later.

"I will take this apartment, and rent the second bedroom in Charlie's place as a studio." Already knowing the answer, she looked at Tom and asked if that was OK. With a nod from Marie Claire, it was done.

Eliza, as she would now be known in Paris, had a place to live, a studio to work in, and a friend who was fluent in French.

Tom invited Marie Claire, and Charlie to dinner. There Eliza would learn all about Tom's Elizabeth and her best friend. Marie Claire seemed to know all about Melinda and seemed genuinely happy that Melinda and Tom were happily in love for all these years. The more Eliza looked and spoke to

Charlie, the more she seemed to like him. By the time Tom flew home, he was feeling much better about his Goddaughter's time in Paris, and a little anxious about Charlie and how much Elizabeth might grow up.

CHAPTER FIFTY-THREE

"I can't believe you talked me into this birthday party!" Tom giggled as he saw Melinda's discomfort. This was an 80th birthday party!

"You'll have fun," Tom said, "and you look so beautiful."

Melinda looked in the full length mirror and had to admit that she was glowing. Tom, still ever so handsome, although he was a lot thinner these days,(in spite of his habit of eating several muffins a day). His treatments had held the progression of the cancer off for quite a few years, but once again it had reared its ugly head. Even though the doctors were unable to eradicate it, there were still new therapies to keep damage down and let him continue with his daily life. He had some pain now, and the meds caused him problems with nausea, he still was able to keep up a great attitude and a fairly robust schedule. For how long was unsure.

Much had taken place over the last 30 years. There were 6 grandchildren, all almost grown up! Elizabeth, still the apple of Poppa Tom's eye. Not that he ignored the others, but there was just something undeniable between the two of them. In spite of his initial meeting with Charlie, he and Eliza were still together although marriage was not something important to either of them.

Scott and Dianna had invested her inheritance wisely and financially were very comfortable. Although they had some ups and downs in their marriage, it seemed as if the things had been smoothed out. Their son, David, became a lawyer, while Elizabeth was sought after as an illustrator. Rob had quite an adjustment period to life with Sarah. At first he was taken aback by Melinda and Tom living practically on top of them. He felt as if he wanted to take her away from this and start a new life together. They talked and talked before their marriage. With a counselor, they were able to lay everything out on the table, no secrets, no resentments. Even after Phil and Judy gave the couple their space and moved into their own place they were still very close, and when the twins were born, Rob was relieved that they were around to help! Melinda and Tom respected their privacy and never just walked in without calling first and again Rob learned just how important it was to be able to lean on people. Within a few months, Rob felt perfectly at home and part of the "crew." The twins, Elijah and Isaac, and two years later, their little sister, Joy, were delivered by C section. Once again, Sarah was sidelined for long gaps from working. She was just too physically exhausted and totally preoccupied for several years! She would however, in time, return to work.

Steven took the role of Big Brother seriously. He also never let them forget that he was the big brother. Through the years he was the protector, defender and general boss over the kids. By the time the younger ones were teens, they mutinied, but still looked up to him and did seek his advice.

Tonight, on this special birthday celebration, Tom looked at Melinda adoringly. "You know tonight would be extra special if you would grant me one wish." Melinda had no idea what Tom was asking for. " He stood in front of her, and said,"I would love to have the honor of you becoming my wife!" Melinda thought she heard wrong, but Tom produced a beautiful ring and handed it to her.

"Now, at this point? Whatever for?"

"I don't have that many wishes left Melinda, this would be the biggest of all."

Melinda thought about it for a second. All the objections she had had over the years were all inconsequential now. "Tom, I would be most honored to be your wife."

The deal was sealed with a kiss, and the ring placed upon her finger.

Melinda thought this was just formality. Tom had a surprise waiting for her. The birthday party was being held at the Jefferson Hotel, the grand old hotel that was a landmark in Richmond. She laughed when she realized she had never been there before. Usually people visiting Richmond made it a must see stop on their first visit.

They pulled up to the valet parking and exited the car. She felt like a princess with her charming prince. She saw some teenagers whispering and pointing to them. They probably looked like two seniors on their way to prom. She cleared her mind and she saw Tom give a thumbs up to Charlene who had a huge smile on her face. Vivi yelled Mazel Tov! Everyone seemed to be in on the wedding secret. The secret of course was on Melinda. Tonight would be a wedding and birthday celebration. When she realized what was happening, Melinda turned to Tom and whispered in his ear, "Pretty sure of yourself, aren't you. Charlene escorted Tom and Melinda to a little empty table set up for the occasion. Charlene had some candles, some wine and some flowers all prepared. She handed Melinda her "bouquet", spoke a few words about love and life.

There was a huge candelabra on the table. On signal, one by one of the people most important and influential in Melinda and Tom's life together came forth, said a few words, and with some tears lit a candle. Dianna led off, with her family, Scott, Eliza,(and even Charlie), and David. Next followed Sarah, Rob, Steven, Elijah and Isaac, and Joy. Vivi and Stan, Judy and Phil, Ken and lastly Charlene.

Tom and Melinda each lit a candle and then lit a third candle with both the flames to signify their union. Charlene recited an affirmation about love and marriage, and then had them each take a sip of wine from the chalice. By the powers vested in her from the state of Virginia, they were wed. The family erupted in cheers and clapping. Poppa Tom, was finally, really Poppa Tom, and Melinda was on cloud nine.

So many pictures were taken that night. As Melinda reviewed the photos some days later she marveled at her dearest friends, her beloved family. She was so happy to have had that last picture taken with everyone all together. One of her most favorite pictures was later framed and presented to her entitled, "The Three Amigos" Charlene Adams, Aviva Wingate, Melinda Smith.

CHAPTER FIFTY-FOUR

Melinda knew it was time to finish her story, she shifted her position in her chair and attention snapped to the present.

"The Captain and Melinda's line of cookies, muffins and donuts, had become so popular in Richmond that Dianna, Vivi and I could no longer deal with it. We sold the company to a commercial baker with the agreement that they would keep the name and the most popular of the original recipes. After the chaotic schedule of years of cranking out the baked goods, the cessation of the business created a deep depression. Of course, it was the least important thing at that point in my life to depress me. In the period of the last seven years, we lost Charlene, Ken, and my dearest Tom. I still can't talk about those last days with him because it just makes me weep.

My world had continued to expand through my children and grandchildren, but my contemporary world was shrinking so rapidly.

About 3 years ago, I sat down, with all my grief and sadness at the kitchen table. I had taken the stone that had sat on my windowsill, and held it in my hands. I turned it over and over watching the sparks embedded in the stone. I realized that I had become what I most feared so desperately that day 30 years ago, an old woman. Of course that day 30 years ago I also feared NOT becoming an old woman. Now that I have arrived at this point in life, I am ok with it. All those people that had played a part in my life, I carry them with me. My business life had obviously ended, but I am so satisfied by what I have accomplished.

Let me just end with these facts. You are here today not just to hear about a successful business woman, and her story. You are here today to realize something much deeper. I was never in any danger of failure. I left my unhappy but comfortable life in NY, with plenty of resources. I was financially secure, I could return to friends and family at any time. I had so many advantages, although I didn't realize it at the time. I had the advantage of a solid education, and white privilege. When I went to buy the house that would be the B&B, no one questioned my ability to pay for it. When I went to lawyers, and accountants, no one was warning me that I was taking on a project that I couldn't afford. I did not need a loan, I did not even need a mortgage. I have recognized the fact that my story is unique because I did not struggle. I realize that as things happened to me, it was quite a fairy tale. The only obstacles I faced were of my own making. I thought all the bad and scary things that happened to me were unique, they weren't. Women go through everything that happened to me everyday, whether it's relationship problems, violence inequality etc. It's because of this I have formed a consulting company to assist women, of all ages, to accomplish their dreams. It is simply called by the initials, CCFW, (consulting company for women). I know that 99 percent of you will never be able to just go out and do what I was able to do, but I don't think you should be hampered in your search and desire to accomplish something that is uniquely you. I think you need someone to listen to your fears and concerns, and someone to give you a hand up when you are down. We hope we have anticipated your needs, and that you take advantage of them. The fee for our service is free. Obviously, you will have to arrange for financing and fees associated with property and licenses on your own, but even there, we might be able to offer some assistance. We hope you avail yourself of our counseling services as well, there is a sliding fee for that but don't let finances prohibit you from inquiring as to what we can do for you. Thank you so much for the opportunity to tell you my story, and thanks to Dr. Wainsworth for giving me the platform to do so. In the back of the auditorium waiting to meet you, and help you are my three representatives, Dianna, Sarah, and Elizabeth. We have literature for you, and of course muffins. Once again, thank you."

There was a round of applause and then a rush of eager women heading to the back of the room. Melinda's eye caught a middle-aged woman still just sitting in her chair. She looked teary eyed, and scared. Melinda motioned for her to come up to the stage and take a seat. As they started to talk, Melinda recognized the drive and fear in the woman's expression. "Ahhh," Melinda thought, "My new project!

EPILOGUE

My Dearest Elizabeth,

I have started this letter to you several times, but had to discard the attempts because it would just cause me to cry, but the letter is necessary and time keeps getting shorter for me to do this. I can never express how much you are loved. Poppa Tom had an exceptionally loving spot for you. We decided that our estates, his and mine, would be revealed after my death. Until then, the money and property were held in a private account. We had stipulations that each grandchild could withdraw money for college and if warranted, graduate studies as well. Other than that, nothing was touched. The estate will now be divided with 10% to your Mother and Father, 10% to Aunt Sarah and Uncle Rob. The remaining 80% will be divided equally among my 6 grandchildren. I am sure no one will contest that Aunt Sarah and Uncle Rob's children are truly my grandchildren. I would be most disappointed if anyone felt differently.

Please know that there are some things that Vivi might want, and those things, whatever they are, should go straight to her.

There is one special thing just for you. The stone on my kitchen windowsill. I had it evaluated not too long ago, and as suspected it is just a piece of turquoise. I have no idea how it appeared in the woods behind the B&B all those years ago. I always thought it was just there for me to find. It does not have much of a monetary value, but to me, it was my talisman. I learned that turquoise is a fairly fragile stone, it should not be exposed to chemicals or soaked in water. I would like you to take it and keep it always. Keep it out somewhere to serve as a reminder of me. Perhaps you will find as I did, that when I needed to work something out, holding it and seeing the sparks of gold shine helped me to think things through. All of us go through trials in our lives, no one is immune. Inequities arise when we aren't allowed or able to rise above our problems or receive help towards a solution. I would also request that you pass it on as I did, to one of my future family, to keep up the tradition. Tell them it's story. That way a piece of me will stay alive.

I wish you the best life has to offer, that your goals and ambitions are realized and that you find love, perhaps you already have!

Your loving Grandmother,
Momma Melinda